Eros Unchained

Dirk Mourningwood

Samantha,
Why? Just... why? Thanks...

Introduction

A wise friend once told me that the best sex you'll ever have isn't that fully loaded Lamborghini Veneno. It's the '91 Honda with no muffler.

I think about that often.

I'm still not sure what it means.

Always practice safe sex.

After that, go wild.

Trigger warnings feel almost unnecessary to include in a book of eight male-on-male erotica stories. Prepare yourself for graphic sexual acts and strong language. The sex isn't always safe; those involved aren't always sober. There are age gaps and power dynamics, but no one is forced in the end.

Contents

Comfy

KYLE AND I WERE inseparable, never seen without the other, until we suddenly were. We were accepted to different colleges, moved away, and drifted apart under the weight of a new life and new social circles. Seven years passed without a text or call, though I thought of him often enough.

Work took me to the west coast, a thousand miles from home, so imagine my surprise one day while I compared the labels of two soup brands when someone slapped my ass. I spun, ready to deck whoever it was, and stopped short when I recognized Kyle's mug grinning at me behind a thick beard. My raised fist shot around him in a bear hug, lifting his short ass off the linoleum floor.

"Kyle! Why...?" was all I could manage when I put him back down.

"I just moved for work. You?"

"Same!"

It turns out Kyle changed his major after his first semester and was just hired by the same company as me. We could have gone to the same school and lost no time together, but we tried not to focus on that.

All our little shared mannerisms instantly clicked back. We pushed our carts side by side, finishing each other sentences, half of which were nonverbal. All the slang phrases known only to us slipped right back into our vocabulary, and I thought nothing of adjusting his shirt's collar, which was flipped and driving me nuts.

Seven years later, no time had passed between us.

"How are you still single?" Kyle asked as we stood next to my car with his ice cream melting.

I shrugged and smirked. "You spoiled me for anyone else."

He rolled his eyes. "I'm sure that's it."

"And what's all this?" I grabbed at his beard with both hands.

He swatted me away. "Go away. You're just jealous."

"Maybe, yeah."

"Dude, what are you doing tonight? Because you should come over to my place. Watch movies or Mario Kart, whatever."

I would have canceled dinner with Hugh Jackman and Lucy Lawless to spend time with Kyle. He texted me his address, dropping it into a chat thread years abandoned.

His ice cream was probably soup by the time we finally parted. When I shut my car door behind me, I finally let myself breathe a long sigh and admitted to myself that the blush across my cheeks and neck was more than the late spring heat.

I learned a lot about myself in the last seven years, including the ability to admit how great Kyle looked in his cargo shorts and tee. He put on a little weight, but that beard... holy damn.

I pulled up in front of his house a few minutes early, grabbed the box of red wine from the back seat, and knocked on the door. Kyle ripped it open within a breath, waving me in. He shifted weight between his feet, antsy as I pulled off my shoes.

"Dude, the last few hours have lasted a year," he said. "I don't care how it sounds. I've missed you." He pulled me into a hug, burying his face in my chest. I returned it just as fiercely, feeling the same. When he asked why I was single, I hadn't lied. I dated plenty of girls through college and boys afterward, but no one compared to what I felt with Kyle—that perfect ease.

We released each other, and he waved me to the stairs beside the front entrance. "My room's upstairs."

I glanced across the living room and kitchen beyond, realizing I assumed this was Kyle's house, not that he rented one room of it. He led us up and to the second door on the left. A bay window on the far wall looked over a sparkling retention pond in the backyard, reflecting glittering light and sweltering heat into the room. The entirety of his life was crammed into the rest of the space. A full-sized bed on the floor, a TV on a dresser, clothes piled in the corners of the shallow closet, and a crooked stack of moving boxes crowding around the window. I knew it was far too early, but I was already thinking about him moving into my two-bedroom apartment.

Kyle shut the door behind us and gestured to the only sitting option, the bed. He pulled two glasses from a cabinet over his dorm fridge, and I poured from the wine box's tap.

"To coincidence," he said, tapped my glass, and hid his grin with a long sip.

For a box of red, it wasn't the worst. Maybe I should have gotten a fifth of Jack instead, or as well. I leaned back on my side, propped up on an elbow. "Movie or video games?"

Kyle waved his glass at the moving boxes. "Or dig through those for the gallon of Jack and get shitfaced?"

Yep, he was reading my mind like no time had passed. "Wine tonight. Jack next time."

He walked across the bed by me, plopped down cross-legged, and took up the remote from his nightstand. "Godfather or Hedwig?"

I choked on my wine. "Well, that's a range!"

"Hedwig, it is." Kyle adjusted himself to the head of the bed, leaning against the wall while navigating the TV menus. I joined him there, shoulder to shoulder, and drained my second glass. He hit play and passed his empty cup. "Top me off."

When I turned to hand back with his glass, Kyle was finishing pulling off his belt. His shorts were unzipped, too.

"Getting comfy?" I asked.

"Yep. Shorts are snug." He chugged half the cup at once. "This gets better the more you have."

"That's how you know it's the good boxed wine." I set my cup on the floor beside the bed and unzipped my shorts, mirroring Kyle.

He watched me do it, ignoring the movie for now. "Getting comfy?"

I reached down for my wine. "Yep."

His eyes narrowed as he bit his lower lip. Kyle finished his wine again, handing me the cup. "More please." His face was getting flushed. When I turned back this time, he was pulling his t-shirt over his head. He flopped back against the wall. "What? It's hot in here."

I poked him in the belly, trying to keep light and playful while my eyes drank in the hair dusting his chest and around his nipples. The last time I saw him shirtless, I'd thought nothing of it. Or I did, but I didn't know why I felt the way I did.

He shied from my poke like it tickled him. "I really want that Jack right about now," he said.

The wine wasn't that strong, but drinking so much so quickly on an empty stomach worked just as well. "Maybe a roommate has something?"

Kyle snapped his fingers. "Smitts! He's got enough to put down an elephant. Be right back." He was out the door before he finished the sentence.

The room was sweltering in the early evening sun, and I looked at the window, noting the thick paint covering the seams. I picked at my shirt once, twice, then set down my empty glass and pulled it off. Kyle rushed back a second later, a bottle of rum in his fist. He shut the door again and crawled across his bed on his knees. His shorts slipped as he did, binding around his thighs, and he toppled forward. He kicked them off with a grunted curse. Wearing only tight, dark trunks, he dropped back at my side. No force on earth could keep me from noticing how his bulge jiggled as he did.

He looked me over quickly, noticing my shirt was off. "Comfier?"

"Well, now I feel like I'm still overdressed."

"That's on you." He touched two fingers to the fish tattoo on my ribs. "Did that hurt?"

I chuckled. "I was stoned out of my mind, so not really." I shook my cup at the rum bottle.

Kyle filled it halfway, then his own.

"I guess I'm staying here tonight."

He tapped his glass to mine. "I guess you are. We got some catching up to do."

I missed that little mischievous smirk and the twinkle in his blue eyes. "And how are you still single?" I asked him.

Kyle chugged a few shots worth of rum and winced. I followed his lead and coughed. It was not good rum.

"Whoa, that's..." He wiped his mouth. "You know how it goes. Have some fun, but no one sticks."

"I guess you'd know if you've found the right person. What was your longest attempt?"

"A few months?" His voice lilted up like a question. He brought the rum back to his lips rather than elaborate.

My mind swam with the wine and rum while my hands felt heavy and clumsy. I looked down into the empty glass. Fucking hell, that was probably six shots worth. How was I not passed out?

Kyle's fingers were on my ribs again, prodding the tattoo.

I leaned back, lifting my hips and pulling off my shorts, struggling with them around my ankles, but Kyle grabbed in a fist them and tossed them toward the door. I settled back beside him, wearing only my boxers.

"Comfier?" Kyle slurred, melting against the wall at the head of the bed. "You're still wearing boxers?"

"What? Do you want me naked?"

"I mean boxers, not something more... good."

"More good?" I looked down at my loose, green plaid underwear, then at his tight black trunks. It gave me an excuse to focus on how he was chubbed, his dick pushed to the left toward his hip. I was glad for the buttoned fly on my boxers else I would have broken free already.

"What's wrong with boxers?" I asked.

"Yeah, but have you tried trunks?" He snapped the elastic at his waist. "So supportive. They keep everything in place."

"Maybe I can afford some with the new job. Underwear's expensive."

"They're so nice. Try a pair, and you'll sell your car for a pack."

"Are you offering?"

Kyle bridged his hips, pulling back the top sheet and slipping under. Once covered, he did it again and a few seconds later was holding his dark trunks over me before dropping them on my chest and rolling to his side to face me.

Well, shit.

I lifted my hips, fanning the sheets to slip under, catching a split-second view of Kyle as I did. I'd seen him naked plenty of times before, but never with his dick hard and pointing directly at me from a nest of dark pubes.

I slid off my boxers and dropped them on his side as he did to me. Kyle snatched and tossed them toward the door.

"Dude!" I yelled without any venom and pulled on his trunks. They were a little snug, but cradling my balls was probably the point. Then I noticed the wetness at the left hip—Kyle's precum. I'm sure I added mine to it. "Yeah, okay, these are nice."

"Not going to model for me?"

"I'm either too drunk or not drunk enough for that."

"Come on, let me see." He pushed at my ribs, urging me out of bed.

I relented, rolled to the floor, and stood. I tried a few of the poses from any Mr. Universe photoshoot and ended by turning around and slapping my ass. Kyle was snorting into his palm the whole time. He tried to keep his eyes on mine, but they wandered over my body. Especially to his trunks and my very obvious erection in them. After a minute, I slipped back into bed. Kyle applauded as I pulled off his trunks, dropped them on his face, and rolled toward him. He tossed them away, leaving us naked under the sheets in the fading evening light.

We talked about our lost time, laying a foot apart and staring into each other's smiling eyes. He'd lived in Japan, South Africa, and Ireland for ten months each, which he blamed for why he could only rent a shithole room now. I told him about the book I'd been trying to finish and my string of failed relationships, careful to keep the pronouns neutral. He told me about his, just as neutral.

The conversation lulled. My arm, which had been resting along my side for so long, itched to reach for him. I leaned toward him, and he met me halfway. My heart threatened to surge through my ribs as our lips met, and his beard brushed my cheeks. His hand slipped over my belly, under my elbow, and across my ribs. I scooted closer, pushing my bottom arm under his neck and the other across his back.

Kyle swung a leg over me, straddling my hips with his elbows on either side of my shoulders. Our chests and bellies pressed together. Our raging erections, too, but we were only focused on the other's eyes and our soft kisses.

Kyle pushed his forehead against mine. "Some cosmic force made us see the world apart, but here we are together again."

My hands moved across his back, holding him against me, his sweat from the room's heat, the alcohol, and our passion mixing with mine. I said something I'd told him often enough years ago but with a deeper meaning now. "I love you, Kyle."

He snorted once and kissed the tip of my nose. "I love you too, Jacob. I feel like all my failed relationships only worked to prepare me for this, to admit what I knew a decade ago. Fuck, dude. I couldn't guess how often I fell asleep thinking about you since college."

I shifted my hips, my dick, against him. "What did we do in these thoughts?"

Kyle shifted to my side, resting his head on my shoulder to look up at me, tossing a knee over my leg to stroke his foot against mine and stretching his arm low across my waist. "This. This closeness. There's nothing and everything between us."

That sounded a lot purer than when I'd fantasized about us.

"Did you imagine us like this?" he asked.

My fingers traced up his arm and down his ribs. "Oh yes."

He kissed my chest and pushed up on his elbow to smile down at me. "And what were we doing?"

We were remarkably lucid, considering how much we'd drank, but I still blurted out what I never thought I'd say to anyone. "Slow and tender, you slipping into me and never taking your eyes off mine as we make love." My fingers on his ribs glided down to his hips and along his length, wiping the drop of precum across his head.

Kyle looked up, eyes going a little off mine.

I rolled toward him, turning his chin to put me back into his focus. When the smile returned to his eyes, I leaned forward to kiss him.

"Sorry," he mumbled. "I..."

"What?"

He squeezed his eyes tight and shook his head. When he opened them again, his grin had fully returned.

"I might have exaggerated my past," he said.

It was a leap, but I knew him enough to take it. "You're a virgin."

He nodded, shutting his eyes around tears. I wiped them away with a knuckle.

"I've been close a few times," he said. "I don't care about sex. I want that connection."

I kissed him again and gripped his cock. "Though, it seems someone else does seem to care about sex."

"Yeah," Kyle chuckled. "That's usually my problem, that he doesn't want to play. I'm not sure I know what to do."

"I'll tell you what you do." I pushed him to his back and got up to my knees. My lips wove a path from his along his neck, collar bone, and focused on his chest a moment before continuing to his belly. Kyle breathed sharply when I grasped his cock, kissed my way around it, and dragged up tongue up his salty sack.

I left my dick ignored for this moment, twenty years in the making, as I slid him into my mouth, and a loud moan escaped his. His fingers tangled in my hair as his breath quickened through clenched teeth. He seized and released within seconds, firing against my throat, and I held him in me, working my tongue around his length, not letting a drop escape.

Body still shivering with aftershocks, he pulled me up to kiss him, his tongue working against mine like he wanted to taste his seed in me. Finally, he pushed his forehead into my chest as he tried to catch his breath.

"We won't regret this in the morning, will we?" he asked. "When we're sober?"

"Absolutely not, Kyle. I've waited decades for this."

"Good. Good."

"You either, right?"

He wiped his nose against me as he shook his head. "I've never had a word for what I am. Maybe I'm a Jacobsexual."

"Demisexual," I corrected him, tracing kisses across his forehead.

With the movie credits rolling, Kyle hovered over my cock, tongue out, as I quickly finished myself. He caught most of my load with a mix of eagerness and anxiety.

We spent the next night in my queen-sized bed and had his single-room lease cleared out before it was renewed at the end of the month.

We must have had the patience of saints because it was weeks before the first time he was lining up his cock with my back entrance.

On our sides, chest to back, his other arm under my neck and around my chest, we couldn't be closer as I slowly exhaled, and he filled me with gentle pressure. The burn was nothing compared to how he pressed against my prostate, making my eyes roll back. Out and back in, just as slowly, just as completely.

"Hold there," I gasped.

Kyle kissed my neck and shoulder but kept his hips unmoving while I savored him in me. Twisting, I focused my breath in and out of my mouth, and he surged forward to kiss me.

"Go," I urged him, and his rhythm restarted, dragging me nearer to climax without even touching myself. His forehead against mine, he sped up, pushing harder, deeper. We'd wanted this first time to be slow, but I could tell by his breathing he wouldn't last much longer.

"Fuck me, Kyle! Cum inside me!"

He growled and surged into me, holding there with the veins in his neck popping and his teeth tight. His cock pulsed in me, over and again, filling me with him. His head dropped to my shoulder as he gasped, trying to catch his breath. I stopped him with a hand on his ass as he started to pull out. Once I was sure he wasn't leaving me, I navigated his hand to my cock, and he got to work. The angle was awkward, it was his off-hand, and I wasn't used to his rhythm, but

I still came within seconds, tightening around him as I shot on the towel spread under me.

I gasped and clenched when he pulled around and maneuvered in front of me, planting kisses across my cheeks, nose, and lips. A big part of me wanted to rush to the toilet and shower to clean up, but a bigger part was utterly content to lay there staring into those eyes without a word said.

I finally broke the silence. "Getting comfy?"

"Very."

On the Clock

IT WAS SOMETHING LIFTED straight from the sticky screenplay of a porn. I woke to a flooded bathroom, called the plumber, and he was now listing off the litany of problems he'd found. The sewer pipe leading to the main line along the road would have to be scoped and possibly cleared of roots from the tree I took down in my front yard last summer. I wanted to ask for a second opinion, but I was already several hundred deep with this guy, with his closed-cropped blond hair and beard. Luckily, it's a good thing to stare at someone's eyes when they're talking because I couldn't take mine off his—a light blue, almost gray.

We were in my kitchen on either side of the island. He took a sip of the tea and leaned forward, folding his thick forearms and giving me a view down his black v-neck uniform with "Mick" embroidered on the breast.

"It's not uncommon in these older houses, Colten," he said, looking up at me. "I did three last year. The trees are finally getting down to the pipes and wrecking them. You should call your insurance. Scoping the pipe will hit your deductible."

My insurance deductible was more than half a month's salary. Were this a porn, I'd ask if there were some other way I could pay, and he'd accept blow jobs and a handy in exchange for twelve thousand dollars worth of pumping. But this wasn't a porn, and plumbers don't accept handjobs for services rendered.

Oh, I'd like to, though. Looking down Mick's shirt, I'd love to run my hands through that chest hair and across his pecs.

"Do you want to get started?" Mick asked, picking up the tea and blowing across it.

Leaning back against the counter, I braced a foot against the edge of the island, giving Mick a view up my loose shorts if he chose to look.

He did.

It was just a flicker—blink, and you miss it glance, but I saw it.

"I guess so." I sighed. "There goes my vacation plans."

"Yeah, I'm sorry. I hate this part of my job, telling people what it'll cost. I could patch the toilet issues, but that's just delaying. What were your vacation plans?" He glanced up my shorts again, taking a longer look from my knee up my thigh.

I shifted my hips, spreading my legs just a little. "I rent a lake cabin once a year for two weeks."

"Yeah?" Sip. "Do you like to kayak and fish?"

"No. There's no one for three miles. I hike and meditate." I waited for him to take another sip. "Naked."

He didn't give me the spit take I'd hoped for, but it was close.

"Nice," Mick said and set down his empty mug. "I've gone skinny dipping, but how different does it feel to leave the house naked?"

"It feels," I dropped my foot to the floor and leaned my forearms on the island close to him. "It sounds cliché but freeing. Natural. I'm usually naked around the house." I picked at my tank top and winked at him.

Mick didn't back away but returned my grin. "You can't be naked for the plumber. Got it."

He hooked a finger around my tank top's front collar and released, letting it snap back.

"If I had known the plumber would be so hot, I wouldn't have worn underwear today," I chuckled, biting my lower lip.

Mick traced a finger around his mug's edge. "I do feel bad about you missing your vacation. Your chance to wander the woods with your dick out."

I was starting to rise from Mick's closeness, but his casual mention of my dick brought me to full attention. "I'll manage, somehow." I slid forward an inch so our forearms were close enough that I could feel his body heat. The hair on his arms tickled mine. My eyes walked up his arms and across the stubble on his jaw. "I've got a question for you," I said. "Either way you answer, it won't affect me hiring you."

His eyes narrowed, and he raised a brow.

"Do you want to have sex?"

Mick snorted, pushing off the island and covering his laugh. He froze, eyes wide, when I wasn't laughing with him. "You're serious?"

I nodded.

"I'm on the clock here."

"You're drinking tea in my kitchen on the clock. I know how it is to be a contractor."

He sputtered a string of failed syllables before managing, "I have other jobs to get to."

"I'm not suggesting a romantic cruise and hours of cuddling."

"What makes you think I'd want to have sex with a man?"

I shrugged. I'd seen him peeking up my shorts. "I'm also not suggesting we get married after."

He leaned his palms on the island. "What are you suggesting, then?"

I glanced toward my living room and back at him. "You relax on the couch while I suck your dick. Maybe I'll ride you."

"Fucking hell, Colten. You don't waste any time getting to the point."

"As you said, you're on the clock. You're hot, and I'd like to see you naked."

He drummed his fingers on the granite for a few heartbeats, then slapped it and tossed his hands up. "Yeah, alright, okay. Nothing gay about getting a BJ, right?"

"Nothing at all." I waved toward the living room. "I just need to grab something." He took two steps backward before turning. I went down the hall to my bedroom. When I returned a moment later with my "go bag," Mick was sitting on the edge of the couch with his elbows on his knees, tapping his fingertips together.

I set my little black bag on the coffee table and pulled a long strip of dark cloth from it. Mick looked up, a little nervous at seeing the blindfold, but he didn't say anything when I sat on the coffee table opposite him. I pulled back my hands from fastening it behind his head and held back my gasp. When I couldn't see his blue-gray eyes, I only wanted to touch his full lips and stroke a knuckle across the stubble on his cheek. His lips parted, and I forced myself to move on.

I put my hands on his shoulders, sensing the strength under that v-neck. Yeah, he had a body under that shirt. He leaned back with the slight pressure I applied, and I let my palms slide down his sides as he moved under me.

My hands kept moving across his front. In stark contrast to me, he wasn't hard. His hands went behind his head when I unclasped his belt buckle, popped the button on his jeans, and pulled down his fly.

No underwear. How fun.

I ran my fingers through his trimmed pubes, then slipped them around the jean's waist and tugged. Mick lifted his hips to help, and a second later, there he was, his chubbed, uncut cock resting on a huge set of shaved balls.

He was on the clock, no time to sit back and admire. I dropped to my knees between his ankles.

My right hand grasped his cock, lifting it to drag my tongue across his smooth balls. Mick sucked in a sharp breath when my tongue shot under his sack. His cock pulsed once in my grip, growing with every pound of his heart. I shifted it into my mouth, wanting to feel it grow with every time I plunged him toward my tonsils.

Mick's fingers slipped through my hair, tightening to a loose fist, guiding me to move slower, to stay down longer, until I was about to choke on him filling me. I came up for air and licked the bead of precum from his head. He pushed me down again, holding me to work my tongue across the underside of his cock.

When next he let up, I lifted his balls to bury my nose under him, licking up his taint, smooth as butter. His aroma alone might have driven me over the edge, a perfect blend of whatever rugged scents were in his body wash and the first hint of how he might smell by the end of a long day's work. Mick's gasp as I ran up his length again fueled me, but his hands shifted to either side of my head, holding me stationary to rock his hips forward, taking direct control of our rhythm. He didn't go as deep, swirling his hips and letting me focus on his crown. His heavy breathing told me my chance to offer something else was limited.

Lifting from his hold, I breathed, "Do you want to fuck me?"

His response was a hummed affirmative as my tongue ran up his length again.

I reached into my bag for a condom and lube. When I turned back, Mick ripped off his shirt with a single-arm maneuver I'd only seen done on the internet. I stood, dropping my shorts and tearing open the rubber as I did. He adjusted his blindfold as I quickly rolled on the condom and placed a knee on either side of his hips. His hands immediately dropped onto my thighs, fingers curling around my hips. With a squirt of lube stroked onto his cock and another around my hole, I eased back, guiding him into me.

He may be on the clock, but I wasn't rushing this step.

The first half-inch is always a shock. He remained a statue beneath me, giving me full command as I exhaled, gently allowing an inch at a time. Timing my breath helped with the burn as he stretched me. Halfway there, the rest went as easily as all the sword and sheath metaphors one could think up. He slid in smoothly, slipping along the spot that made my eyes roll back. I raised up with just as much care, and Mick pulled off the blindfold. His fingers traced down my ribs on the way down to grasp my cock and smear the precum across my head with his thumb. With a hand in his chest hair, I rocked my hips, grinding his cock against that perfect spot. I didn't have to ask if he liked it, by how he gasped for air with his lips parted.

Mick's hands slipped under my tank top, rubbing calloused fingers up my back, then down to grab the hem and pull it over my head. One hand stayed at my lower back, but the other returned to my cock, stroking its length. His hips mirrored my motion, and I slowed to let him take over.

Fucking hell, every thrust hit me at that perfect angle, bringing me closer to climax faster than him working my dick.

I wouldn't stand much longer under his assault and leaned forward, sliding a hand behind his neck, and kissed him. His tongue grazed mine as he whispered, "Are you close?"

His cock made speech impossible. I could only nod my head against his and bite my lower lip.

Suddenly, he was a fucking jackhammer against my ass, decimating my prostate. The orgasm started in that space behind my balls, seized up my spine, and I grabbed a fistful of his chesthair as I shot onto him and beyond, hitting the couch behind. At the same time, he shoved deep into me and held, and I felt his cock pulse in me as he filled the rubber.

I fell forward, and we could only pant against each other's ears.

Finally, I pushed back upright. "I'll get the towel."

His hand shot behind my neck, pulling me back onto him for a deep kiss, his tongue gliding across my lips before releasing me.

I dismounted with a gasp and grabbed the hand towel from my bag. Before I could offer it to him, Mick wiped my cum from his chin, looked at it, then put his finger completely into his mouth, pulling it out slowly without breaking eye contact.

Tossing the condom on the coffee table, I draped the towel over my mess on his chest and stomach and mounted him again. "Not gay, huh?" I kissed him on the neck, the cheek, the lips, and flicked my tongue on the tip of his nose.

"I never said I was or wasn't."

"Ass. You were just fucking with me, then."

Mick waved his hands over me. "Very literally." He bobbed up to kiss me. "Now that these pipes are drained, I'd like to use your shower real fast, then get to work on the ones I came here for."

Bottom Bunk

"YOU DON'T NEED THAT, baby. I trust you."

Jon laid back and spread his legs wider, lifting his hips to show me his asshole. The very fact that he'd say that when this was our first date only made me see the need for the condom even more. I fumbled with the packaging, trying to find the perforated edges. I finally gave up and used my teeth to tear it open and rolled it onto my dick with one hand.

"Fuck me, baby," Jon moaned and wiggled closer.

Did he know my name? Did that matter? With a squirt of lube, hindered by the cramped space in my bottom bunk, I slid into him. He moaned and growled, bucking his head back and wrapping his legs around me.

"Fuck me, baby!" he gasped between thrusts. "Rail me with that hot cock!"

Yeah, he didn't know my name. Whatever.

I pulled out, flipped him over, and yanked his hips up. Standing beside the bunk bed, I fucked him as hard and fast as I could while he moaned and bit the pillow with every thrust. Gripping his hips until my nails bit into his skin, I forced myself deeper. That familiar ache signaled from my balls; I wouldn't last much longer.

Then, I plateaued.

Jon sounded just as eager as I kept slamming into him, but I wasn't getting any closer. Since my roommate moved out last semester, abruptly ending our unique sexual relationship, I'd had a string of college boys to fuck. After all, I had the room to myself. I could host.

Thinking of Raj pushed me forward just enough, and I shot into the condom. Toppling forward onto Jon's back, I offered him a few more thrusts before pulling out. He immediately rolled over, shifting close enough to yank off the condom and plunge my cock into his mouth. Still ultra-sensitive from my orgasm, I flinched away from his efforts, but he hung on while working himself with one hand and the other disappearing between his legs to keep playing with his ass. He came within seconds, oozing a few thick globs that he caught in his palm.

With one fist full of cum, he reached for his shirt on the floor. "That was great, baby." He had his clothes gathered and disappeared into the bathroom.

I considered my string of hookups while searching for the condom. The supply of college bottoms seemed... bottomless... but they rarely came back, or were invited, a second time. Was that really a bad thing? It might be a goal to fuck a single person long-term, but until then, I'd keep my dresser's top drawer full of lube and rubbers.

I was sitting on the edge of the bottom bunk, wearing only my briefs, when Jon popped his head in. "DM me. Let's do that again, baby."

A weak smile was all I could offer him; being called "baby" was now high on my list of turnoffs. I might message BigBoiJon, but he was only a step over masturbation. SlightlyBelowAverageBoiJon was more like it.

Goddamn, I'd changed quickly with the floodgates that Raj ripped open when he left. Three months brought me from a nervous voyeur, never having touched another man, to being bored by hot college guys eager to let me deep dick them. I had to jerk off twice earlier in the day and pray to the gods I could still get up and last more than a few strokes when I started. Now, I sometimes thought about my unfinished Calculus homework. This couldn't be healthy. I grabbed my phone and texted the one person who might help.

"Fuck you, Marsh! The next time you're bored with a hottie, send him my way." Samantha huffed and crossed her arms on the treadmill beside mine.

"I don't think you have the equipment they're looking for, dear."

"You haven't seen what's in my nightstand drawer," she chuckled. "Seriously, the only one taking care of me is me. Meanwhile, you're going through more six-inchers than a Subway at lunch."

"Much like the sub shop, they're often more like confident four and a halfs."

"Marsh! You're a fucking size queen now? You bitch!"

"Takes one to know one."

Samantha opened her mouth for a retort but shrugged instead. "So your fledgling sex drive has sputtered. How do we fix this?"

I was glad to have her to talk to, but it sounded weird having my problem reduced so easily. "It was easy with Raj. I always felt like I wanted more."

"Raj was a prick. He wanted you to worship him. You only wanted more because he kept everything from you."

She wasn't wrong.

"Tell me," Samantha said, "do you have any closeness with these guys? Kiss and touch and cuddle and make dinner plans and that gay shit? Or is it all blowjobs and buttfucking?"

Goddamn, I loved her.

"A guy last week wanted me to eat his ass. Does that count?" I asked.

She glared at me. "And did you?"

"Of course."

"Why didn't you tell me about that sooner? Rude. Put a pin in that. I need to hear more." She sighed. "I couldn't imagine it personally, but maybe you need a break from raw sex. Maybe you need someone to hold hands with and go to a movie. Someone to hang out with while you both do homework."

"We've held hands." I reached for hers, but she pulled it from me.

"Someone you also sometimes fuck. I mean a relationship, Marsh."

"Isn't that what I've been trying to do?"

She rolled her eyes. "You said Jon didn't know your name even after you nutted in his ass. Try starting something as friends."

Finding a hookup was simple, but friends? "And how do I do that?"

"We're in college. Talk to a classmate in person, not on an app. Join a club."

I stood in the quad, staring at the poster board covered with fliers, debating between the Fermentation Club and Urban Explorers. The first would be all organic chemistry majors making weird shit, so I scanned the QR code for the second and was dropped into a chat message in the app I used for my hookups. I'd almost forgotten it has other, more legitimate uses.

MarshMellow: Hey, I saw your flier about the Urban Explorers club?

UrbanLens: Great! Have you done any exploring before?

MarshMellow: Not really

UrbanLens: Np. We're checking out St Aurelia this Saturday at 4pm. Meet us there out front. Pack like a hike. Wear sturdy jeans and shoes.

Well, that was easy. We'd introduce ourselves with actual names in person. I had to poke around a bit to find out where St. Aurelia was, a long-condemned church verging on a cathedral a quick bus ride away. A news article said it was scheduled for demolition next month. I only owned two pairs of jeans and one set of sneakers, so my wardrobe essentially chose itself. When I got back to my apartment and into my bedroom, I gagged at the smell, reeking of musk and sex. I spent the rest of the afternoon cleaning and went to the laundry mat that evening. I kept my back to the storage room that Raj and I always let ourselves into.

With the notebooks dumped from my backpack and replaced with two water bottles and a handful of jerky, I got off the bus and walked three blocks to the church. Two college guys were waiting on the curb. One with short, curly hair flailed his arms and yelled at the other.

"This is our thing, Jorge! You can't keep inviting strangers!"

"Don't you want to share this with others?" said Jorge.

They started, and both looked me up and down as I approached.

"You must be him," said the curly-haired guy.

"I messaged you, I think? I'm Marshal." I offered a hand forward for whoever would accept it.

Jorge took it in a warm, firm grip. "Hey Marshal. I'm Jorge."

I looked down at his hand, following up past the tangle of bracelets, along his arms rippling with muscle just beneath the dark skin, noting the professional-grade camera hanging from his neck, and up to the smile he flashed.

"And I'm leaving," said the other man, turning on a heel.

"Miko, wait," Jorge called after him but didn't give chase. He only tightened a fist and huffed a deep sigh.

I wasn't going to ask about that. Not yet. "Is it just us?"

Jorge blew out a loud breath and turned back to me. "Looks like it. It's hard to keep members with Miko."

I looked past him to the old church. Crumbling spires and arches thrust skyward that looked to be half held up by the vines growing through the mortar. "Is it safe to go in with just two of us?"

He waved down my worries. "Oh yeah. I've been in here a few times. Just walk carefully." He led me to the chainlink fence, disregarded all the danger and no trespassing signs, and pulled open a loose flap. "Sorry we're starting so late. I had classes and work. There's still a few good hours of light."

"What do we do?" I craned my neck back to the high bell tower in front. The gaping hole over the main entrance glinted with a few shards of stained glass still remaining in its frame.

"We usually just wander urban ruins, looking for places to set up photoshoots, but I have a mission today," said Jorge, leading us through the thick bushes around the side of the cathedral. "There are rumors of a wine cellar beyond the catacombs. The catacombs were cleaned out a year ago after the new landowners cleared this place for demo, but they didn't find the wine." He stopped beside a piece of plywood leaning against the stone wall and pushed it aside, revealing a window in the stonework. Beyond, the space looked well-lit from the high windows and score of holes in the roof. The floor seemed solid enough, though it was littered with rotted pews.

I swallowed hard. "We go in there for wine?"

"Not for the wine. For the adventure of searching for the wine." Jorge had a leg over the window, then dropped in and offered me a hand. I didn't need it, but I accepted it to feel his warm fingers again. "Though, if we find it, we'll drink it." He winked.

An odd pit sank in my gut as I walked into the center of the room. With the din of traffic and the city melting away, the silence hummed like a pressure in my ears so accustomed to always having the city's background noise.

"You feel it too, don't you?" Jorge whispered from my side. "That island of quiet is one reason why I love doing this. Condemned and forgotten places always feel quieter; like the ghosts are trying to drown out the world."

I imagined what the place looked like in its full glory, but it was difficult, as everything of value or interest had been removed, looted, smashed, or tagged decades ago. Now, it was just a rotted husk shaped like a very large church.

"The stairs down are by the chapel in the back right," said Jorge, pointing. I followed, picking my way around the debris. He stopped to squat, brushed through the mess as if noticing something of interest, then stood and brushed his hands on his jeans. He didn't find anything, but it gave me a great view of how his ass filled out his pants.

"So, you and Miko?" I let my question hang.

Jorge nudged some old wood away with his shoe. He sighed. "Miko wants us to be exclusive in everything, including hobbies. They're a very controlling person."

I noted the pronoun usage. "You're not an item?"

Jorge snorted. "No."

"Why do you put up with that?"

"They weren't always like this. Here's the stairs."

Jorge took a flashlight from his backpack and handed me a second. As we descended, the wide stone stairs slowly curved to the left before depositing us in a narrow tunnel with a low ceiling. Jorge's light played over the empty niches and stone sarcophaguses with their lids shoved aside.

"They moved the bodies," I said, peering into one. "Like in Poltergeist. Or, I guess not like in Poltergeist... How does that work? Is the land still consecrated?"

Jorge shrugged. "Sounds like you already know more about it than me." He led us through cramped paths that kept ending in deadends of collapsed rubble, grumbling each time. "The place is falling down on itself. This was all clear the last time I was here."

"We're not lost, right?" I wiped my hands across the sarcophagus lid to my right, trying to make out the name and dates.

"Of course not," Jorge chuckled. "Wait, though." He dropped to a squat, raised his Nikon, adjusted the lens, and aimed it toward me. "Touch that again like you were."

I did and tried not to smirk while he enthusiastically snapped a dozen pictures.

"Squat down with your back against the stone. Perfect. Now, tilt your head up. Love it. Close your eyes."

I followed along with his directions. I didn't expect to be a model today, but I didn't hate the attention.

He sat beside me, leaning his back against the tomb. "This isn't just about exploring and finding neat little treasures, Marshal. I sometimes just like to lose myself in the place, imagine what it would be like to exist when the place was active."

I rolled from my squat to sit beside him, hips almost touching, legs stretching to the far wall. "How do you do that?"

He clicked off his flashlight.

I clicked off mine, plunging us into total darkness. The catacomb smells rose quickly, a mixture of dampness and something earthy, but also Jorge's cologne or body wash or deodorant. I hadn't noticed before, but he smelled wonderful. Sounds came next; a distant drip and Jorge's breath beside me, though my heartbeat rose to pound in my ears. The heat radiating from the man beside me... Something moved at my hip, and I flinched but realized just as quickly that it was Jorge's fingers sliding across my jeans. I snatched his hand and squeezed, unsure how I felt about getting fresh in a crypt. Maybe he was reaching to touch me in a shared quiet moment and meant nothing sexual by it. My dick had no qualms about anything as it rose with every thunderous heartbeat, sitting there holding hands in the absolute darkness surrounded by the empty tombs of the long dead.

Maybe not total darkness. Farther down the path we'd been following, a fine line of ghostly green light shone across the hall, only noticeable as my light-starved eyes yearned for something to do. I studied it, convincing myself that it was real. Maybe there was a crack in the wall there?

Jorge brushed the inside of my forearm with his other hand.

"Do you see that light?" I whispered.

Jorge paused his stoking. "What is that?" he asked after a few breaths. He stood, still holding my hand, and pulled me up after him. He pressed the back of my hand against his crotch as he did, letting me feel he was as hard as me. Crypts be damned, I was about to drop back to my knees, fish his dick out of his pants, and blow him right there, but the tunnel flooded with a dim red from his flashlight, and he pulled me after him. A portion of the wall had collapsed, revealing a chamber behind lit by soft green light.

"I think this is the original chapel the cathedral was built over," said Jorge, dropping my hand to crawl through the tight space. I followed, knowing it might be my stupidest idea ever, but that didn't stop me.

Mosaic stained glass shone with the setting sun behind it on one wall, illuminating the small chapel a dozen feet on a side.

"This is better than the wine," Jorge said, getting his camera ready. "Could I get some more photos with you?" He moved to put me between him and the glass.

I posed, trying to look contemplative as would be appropriate for the location, knowing I'd be nothing more than a silhouette without the flash.

Jorge came back toward me. "The lighting is perfect in here. I wonder where this is that the glass is undamaged." He stared at me, biting his lip. He looked perfect in that green light, leaving half his face in shadow. "Would you mind a few more?"

I shrugged, and he snapped away. Then, he paused, looking down at the display on the back of his camera.

"What if you took off your shirt and shoes?" he asked. "I love that look of wearing only jeans."

There it was. Just like blowing Raj in the laundromat storeroom, the little exhibitionist spark within me flared, longing to get my dick out in a public place, even as secluded as we were now. Quid pro quo, though.

"Would you take off yours, too?" I asked.

"Sure." He shrugged off his backpack and pulled off his shirt, revealing a trim waist and smooth chest. I'd fucked a lot of guys in the last few months and seen a lot of dicks, but something about watching him in his low-rise jeans hopping on one foot to pull off his shoe struck me in a very different way. If we'd started this a little differently, if I wasn't still trying to figure out Miko's position in this, this would have made a great first date. And like with any respectable first date, we were now finding coy ways to get each other naked. This wasn't the express route of a hookup.

My toes ground in the loose dirt and debris as Jorge directed me to sit down, hugging my knees. He snapped away, telling me how great these would be.

I was no longer thinking about the place collapsing around us as I moved with Jorge's direction. Bite your lip. Look pensive. Try not to laugh. Brush back your hair.

"Stand up and act like you're going to take off your pants," he said.

I'd play along with that. I hopped to my feet, fingers poised over my button fly, then the zipper. The camera shutter echoed across the old chapel.

"Stay right like that," Jorge said.

I had a thumb in my waistband pushing down and the other holding my zipper at the bottom of its track.

Jorge snapped a dozen more, then moved close enough to brush my hair back. His fingers slowed around my ear. The light through the stained glass highlighted the tiny flecks of green at the edge of his blue irises. God fucking hell I wanted to—

He kissed me.

It was quick, his fingers gripping around the hair on the base of my neck as his tongue licked across my upper lip.

He backed away just as fast, fingers brushing across his lips. "Sorry, I've been wanting to do that."

I wanted to carefully set his expensive camera aside, then throw him to the rubble for an hour of passion, but Samantha's suggestion echoed through my brain: start as friends. What a shit idea. Fucking bitch.

I managed to stay in place and just grin as I put a hand on his shoulder, letting it slide down his bicep and forearm to slip around his fingers. "Me too."

He bit his lip like he was holding back a smile. "Have you posed for boudoir before?"

I looked down at our hands, still intertwined. "Nudes? Not really."

"Boudoir isn't nudes. Well, you're often nude, but you don't show anything. They're tasteful. Classy."

I thought of the extreme closeup shot I took of my butthole to send to a guy, the last and only one to get to date three. Definitely not classy. "Oh, no."

"Want to?" He licked his lips.

"Are these for your personal spank bank?"

He chuckled and crossed his heart. "I promise no one else will see them. You can take what-ever photos you want of me on your phone as collateral or blackmail."

Photography-based foreplay in an ancient, forgotten chapel lit by the setting sun through stained glass. I hadn't been so hard with my pants still on in a long time.

"Turn around. If this is classy, you can't see all of me." I let go of his hand and twirled a finger. "Not yet."

Jorge was grinning wide but turned away as requested. I tore off my jeans and briefs, spotted wet with precum. Giving my cock a quick squeeze and stroke, I folded my hands modestly before me, careful to cover everything.

"I'm ready."

Jorge turned and choked back a gasp, but his eyes landed on mine rather than running all over my body. "Perfect. Lean against that pew over there. Yes, good. Now, turn away a bit more, yes. Let your hands drop."

I turned a little more, giving Jorge my full ass but keeping my erection hidden. The shutter clicked behind me. "This is perfect, Marshal. We're losing the light. We can get a great silhouette. Stand facing the glass, away from me, feet two shoulder widths apart, hands out, fingers spread. Perfect. Yes. This is so hot. Now, hands behind your head."

He directed and praised me, but I wanted to look him in the eyes. "What about the one like I did sitting, holding my knees?" I asked over my shoulder.

"Yes!"

I swept my foot across the ground, clearing the debris, then spun and sat in a single motion to face him. I was still just as hard, wiping precum across my belly as I hugged my knees. He stalked forward, snapping a dozen photos, with an obvious bulge in his jeans. He squatted beside me.

"When can I take my pictures?" I asked, looping a finger around the camera strap.

"I guess before the light's gone." He set down his camera and stood, fingers moving to his fly.

I stopped him with a hand on his, shooting to my feet. I expected him to look down at my body and cock, as all the college hunks did, but he kept his eyes on mine. Eyes twinkling with a thousand hues in the odd light through the stained glass. My other hand slid up his arm, around his shoulder, and down his lower back to pull us closer. My cock grazed the back of his hand, but still he held my gaze. My hand at his belt moved around his to undo the button and zipper. His slipped around my cock, holding it gently with a slow tug as the other moved behind my neck. He pulled us closer, chest to chest, and kissed me. Slow and gentle, with the same tender energy as he gave to my dick.

His jeans finally shook free, and I plunged a hand into his trunks, shivering with that first touch of something new. Jorge was as hard and wet as me. We felt about the same size but he was uncut, and his foreskin made working his shaft effortless. By how he moaned and gasped between our kisses, my efforts were working for him. Focusing on him was all that slowed my path to climax. His lips moved from mine, across my cheek, and to my ear. His warm exhale sent a shiver down my spine, and his tongue across the shell of my ear made me grip his cock harder. My other hand slid into his trunks to squeeze his ass, then around to cup his balls, clenched high with his arousal.

With him at my ear, my nose was in his neck. I trailed kisses across his collarbone and breathed in the scent of his skin. Somehow different than all the men I'd fucked in the last months, he was like a foreign herb.

If Jorge were any of the men in my bottom bunk, I'd have a rubber on with my balls slapping his ass by now. Instead, he was kissing across my jawline, pulling a hand through my hair to guide my head, tilting it to create his path.

In spite of... or maybe because of... his slow attention to my cock, I felt the tension building, drawing me closer to a cliff I wasn't ready to jump off of yet. Jorge seemed in no rush, and I wanted this to last.

I dropped to a squat, pulling my cock from his hand and ripping his trunks down so that his dick slapped me in the nose. After a deep breath of his herbal musk, I lifted his cock and dragged my tongue from his balls and up his length before plunging him into my mouth. Fucking hell, the taste of him, with just a little tang of sweat from our hike through the cathedral. His hands were on either side of my head, drawing my attention up to see him looking down at me, breathing in short pants through parted lips.

There was nothing ungentle about how he pushed his hips forward, stopping when he hit my tonsils. Out and back, always holding my attention on his eyes.

"I'm close, Marshal," he gasped. "Is this okay?"

I nodded and stuck out my tongue to slide along the underside of his length. Without a change in tempo or breath, he exploded against the back of my throat, gagging me with a volume I had to take in three swallows. It was tinted with that same herb as though it ran in his blood. His hand tightened in my hair with his last spasm, and then he was down in front of me, kissing me with a hard passion he hadn't shown before, driving his tongue into my mouth.

"Your turn," he said, biding me to stand with pressure against my sides. His head was leaned back, tongue out, and mouth open by the time I was ready. I stroked hard and fast, but the eagerness in his eyes was what brought me back to the edge of that cliff.

Jorge licked his lips. "Give it to me, Marshal."

I did.

Pitching forward as the waves buckled my knees, I shot across his cheek, nose, and neck, everywhere but his waiting tongue. He ran a finger across his chin and into his mouth.

He stood, grabbing his trunks as he did, and used them to wipe my cum from his face.

"Is this the standard urban exploration experience?" I asked, leaning forward to kiss him.

"Not generally," he chuckled and nodded at my pile of clothes. "You haven't taken a blackmail photo yet."

I dug for my phone and took three. He put a hand behind his neck, flexing his bicep for the full-body shot with his dick hanging limp from a nest of trimmed pubes. I stood hip to hip with him for the second, reaching my arm out for a selfie, angling down to get us head to foot. For the last, I asked him to kiss me, and he grabbed my face with both hands to do it.

I scrolled between the photos in my camera roll, knowing I'd use them to beat off a dozen times in the next week. "What does 'not generally' mean?" I asked. "How often do you have sex on these?"

His smile turned serious. "Never."

"Do you want to get some dinner?"

His smile returned, and he nodded.

"And just like that, you have a boyfriend."

"I have a boyfriend," I beamed back at Samantha.

"I swear to Christ, Marsh, all the men in this college are gay. You're tripping over dick and end up with a cutie like Jorge while I'm going through a pack of batteries a week."

"Maybe you need to join a club." I winked.

Mirror

HANDS CUPPED AROUND HIS hips, knees between his. My form looked perfect in the mirror with his face buried in the pillow. I flexed a bicep, and the results of my pushup challenge were clear. Fuck I looked good fucking him. I should have set up my phone to record. I could definitely beat off to this later. The power flowed like a wave, from my shoulders, through my chest and abs. My ass dimpled with the flex of each thrust.

His moans and grunts timed with my strikes. Deeper, harder. I'd make him feel this in the morning. My fingers ran through the hair on the back of his head, gripping tightly. I wanted to hurt him. Not pain that would last but that he would remember. His memory would record it with the pleasure I pumped into him, intertwining the two.

I pushed his hips down to the bed, pressing my sweaty chest to his back, biting at his shoulders and the back of his neck, working my pelvis in deep, eager motions.

The mirror confirmed my perfect angle and flawless rhythm. Fuck, I could cum just watching that reflection. The familiar tension started deep in my balls. It was too late to stop. My rhythm studdered, faltered, as my cock surged and flexed, firing my seed into the rubber.

Panting, coated in sweat, I pulled out and dropped back to sit on my heels.

He looked back, then rolled over.

"Did you finish?" He asked. I noted his cock was barely half hard.

"Yeah. Didn't you... Don't you want to cum too?" I reached for his cock, but he was already swinging his legs off the bed.

"I'm good, Kevin. Thanks."

"Calvin," I corrected toward the closing bathroom door.

The mirror reflected a sad kid, naked and alone in a prostitute's posh apartment. Well, was Harry a prostitute if I didn't pay him? I used to pay him but hadn't in a month. He never asked for more, I stopped offering, but the sex kept happening. Was it charity? Was he writing off the time on his taxes?

I smirked at the thought. It didn't matter. While my housemates were out at the bars desperately trying to bring home a girl to maybe touch a boob, I was dumping my load in the sexiest man I'd seen. Did it matter that he never remembered my name and hadn't let me see him cum in over a month?

I cleaned off my dick in the sink outside the bathroom and gathered up my clothes scattered across the room. Harry let me give him a strip show when I first arrived. He seemed to like it, if maybe he was a little tired.

"I'm gonna take off, Harry. See you next week?"

There was no immediate response.

"Hold up, Kevin," he yelled when my hand was on the doorknob.

He came out a moment later, wearing his little trunks, and washed his hands in the sink. "Are you up to anything this weekend?"

"I... What?" I watched the flex of his triceps as he scrubbed his hands. "Classwork, but not really. Why?"

Harry snatched a hand towel and turned, leaning his buttock on the counter. "I have a thing and need a plus one."

"A thing?"

"Not a big thing. Just a hang out with drinks. You in?"

I didn't want to agree without knowing more, but neither did I ever want to decline him. Decline Harry once, and there may not be another chance. Or he might remember to restart my payments.

"Sure, yeah. What time?" I asked.

"Saturday, nine. I'll pick you up."

"What should I wear?"

He looked me over and absently grabbed himself, adjusting. "That's fine."

I looked down at my T-shirt and jeans; they were nothing special. "Okay. I'll see you Saturday, then." My hand was on the doorknob again.

"One more thing," he said, drawing me back. Harry pushed off the sink and slid one hand behind my neck. He was close, focusing his hazel eyes on mine. "If you have a good time, I thought we might change our arrangement."

He was close enough that I could lean forward just a few inches and kiss him. "What kind of changes? You don't like our weekly, um, hangs?"

"We can talk more later."

I glanced down his body. My cock surged, seeing his defined outline behind his underwear. I saw him naked every week, but he didn't seem to care much about me touching him. Harry was a sex worker with a lot of rules.

He said my clothes were fine, but I still ripped apart my closet and dresser, hoping to find something nicer without looking like I was trying too hard. I settled on a button-down shirt, my newest pair of jeans, and my cleanest Converse. I even undid the top three buttons of the shirt to show off my necklace. Harry drove up right on time, eyeing me over as I slipped into the passenger seat of his convertible.

"You look nice, Kevin."

"You too." He was wearing all black, but it wasn't a lie. Harry would look great in rags.

"This is just a little party a friend put together. A few of my clients will be there, but you shouldn't have to do anything except have a few drinks and enjoy yourself."

"Past clients? Like... me?"

Harry shot me a confused look that quickly softened. "What does that mean?" he laughed.

"Like... johns."

"Like what?"

"You know... clients?"

He blinked. "Clients I've done taxes for. I'm an accountant."

Holy fuck, he was writing me off on his taxes!

"That's part of what I wanted to talk to you about, Kevin." He reached past my knees to the glove compartment, took out an envelope, and dropped it on my lap. "I never asked why you shoved money at me when we first met, but I was too embarrassed and confused to decline it."

I pulled open the envelope stuffed with cash. "My friend said you were a... were a prostitute."

Harry chuckled. "This was Chuck? He's a dick-head. Of course he'd tell you that."

"But all your rules. You don't let me touch you, and half the time, I don't even think you're enjoying it. And you never get my name right."

"Your name?"

"You call me Kevin. My name is Calvin."

Harry's jaw dropped. "Why didn't you correct me?"

I started to protest that I had every time, but maybe those were mumbled complaints as he was walking away.

"It's April, tax season, and I'm an accountant," he continued. "Of course I'm exhausted when we meet up. And I have rules? I just... It's not that I don't want you to touch me, I just don't think about it. I want to make sure you're taken care of. It's never mattered as much to me about getting off. Don't think I haven't noticed how you're checking yourself in the mirror the whole time."

I fiddled with the envelope, tracing a finger along the edge. The first few times we'd met up felt like dates with dinner and drinks before the clothes came off. How fucked was it that we just flowed into a hookup on a repeating calendar event? If I hadn't gone in thinking he was pay for play, Harry the Accountant, with his abs and bouncy hair, might be my boyfriend. And what kind of sexuality was that, where he didn't need to finish himself off? "So, what's with this party?"

"I'm hoping it's a chance for us to start over, Kev—Calvin." He put a hand on my thigh and squeezed.

"I think we need that." Leaning over, I slipped a hand behind his neck, pulling him toward me. His tongue glided against mine as I breathed in what he breathed out. We hadn't kissed much in the last month, but we took our time over the center console in front of my rented house for almost twenty minutes before Harry pushed back, wiping his mouth, but grinning.

"We'll be late," he said. "More of this later, yeah?"

I nodded and reached across to his lap, squeezing the tight bulge in his black slacks.

We didn't say much else during the half-hour drive. The houses got larger, with taller columns and sturdier stone walls around the property lines. He pulled up to a lakeshore house with the gate swung inward and parked along with the other dozen cars. Faerie lights strung high in the backyard and soft jazz created a mellow ambiance for those wandering in their cocktail dresses or polos and slacks, drinks in hand. I looked down at my outfit, feeling rumpled and cheap like everyone there would see me as a Gap price tag with an orange clearance sticker pasted over my forehead.

"I don't know, Harry. I'm a poor college kid; I don't belong here."

"We should at least pop in for one drink." He leaned over the center console, putting a hand on my thigh.

I looked down at his fingers tracing a slow swirl on the denim. "I don't know. I didn't know what to expect here, but this is..." I looked back at the classy, rich party. "A lot."

Harry pulled his hand away but turned more fully toward me in his seat. "Okay. We're starting over. This is our first date. What do you want to do? Movie? Dancing? Star gaze on the beach?"

We ended up on the far side of the lake with the smooth jazz drifting across the water to us. We put the convertible's top down, leaned the seats back, and opened the bottle of expensive bourbon Harry had intended for the party. We sipped straight from the rim, fingers touching far more than needed as we passed it back and forth.

"You really thought I was a prostitute this whole time?"

"You really didn't guess that?"

He shrugged and handed me the bourbon. "Would a prostitute do this?" Harry pushed over the console and ran the tip of his tongue up my ear. His left hand splayed wide on my stomach, then slipped beneath my belt, giving my dick and balls a firm squeeze.

I tried to maintain my cool even as blood surged southward. I could sense the game developing. "Yes, I think a prostitute would do exactly that."

"What about this?" His hand slid upward, under my shirt and out the neck hole, turning me to face him with a thumb against my jaw. He wetted his lips and pressed them to mine, gentle and tender. Then my chin, following my jawline, and down my neck to my collarbone.

I exhaled slowly, savoring the tingling in my fingertips from his slow kisses. "They might. I haven't been with enough prostitutes to know for sure."

Harry hummed and leaned back against the door with a grin. "What can I do to convince you I'm not a sex worker?"

"Just sit back."

It was my turn to cross the center console. One hand cradled his side, squeezing his firm obliques, and the other popped the top button on his shirt. I kissed the hollow between his clavicles and popped the next button, working my way down.

"I don't know what this proves, Calvin, but I'm listening."

I pushed his shirt open with my nose, giving his nipple a gentle bite. His back arched as I kissed my way through the short hair to his navel, breathing in his woody body wash. I tugged his belt down a few inches to kiss across his waist, my wrist pressing against his erection straining for attention.

I kissed my way back to his lips.

"I want you inside me, Harry. I want it slow and..." I almost said the L-word.

"Does you bottoming for a change prove anything about me?" He smirked and chuckled but quickly bit it back, sensing my serious tone. He cleared his throat. "Yeah, yeah, I want that. Not breaking eye contact, wrapped in each other's arms the whole time."

"We cum at the same time, me shuddering around your cock as you fill me."

Harry's fingers slipped through my hair, tugging me to press his forehead to mine, his breath tickling my lips. "We could do it right here, under the stars."

I pulled back a fraction. God fucking dammit. Why couldn't real life be like the pornos where men could fuck all day without an ounce of preparation? I hadn't bottomed in a while and hoped I could live up to the expectations I was setting. Definitely not without following the proper procedures. "I, uh... How about back at your place?"

The drive back to Harry's apartment felt like it took forever. I played with his dick through his slacks the whole time. At a red light, I unzipped him, wanting to blow him the rest of the way, but he stopped me, saying it wasn't safe while driving. Fucking boyscout. The front of my jeans was soaked with precum by the time we fell through his front door, wrestling each other's shirts off.

I excused myself before the pants came off. It felt weird to use another man's preparation equipment, but I didn't have a choice. Twelve minutes later, he had the electric fireplace started and two glasses of red poured as the same smooth jazz from the party tinkled from the speakers scattered across his place. My breath caught when he turned to me, wearing only his tight black slacks, offering me a glass.

"To first dates." He chimed his crystal against mine.

We each took a sip, eyes boring into each other. We knew what we wanted, but I needed something else first—an answer.

"Why me?" I asked.

Harry's brow wrinkled, and I felt our combined passion cool.

"I like you, Calvin."

"But you're..." I waved my free hand across the opulent apartment, then down his toned pecs and flat stomach.

"None of our differences matter unless we let them." He closed the distance between us, pushing my glass aside and pressing his forehead against mine. His breath tickled my lips. "I've thought about you constantly since we met, but I realize now we both thought the other was something different. We could cut and run, but I only want to stay and know the real you."

"I thought you were a prostitute. What did you think I was?"

"I thought you were soft quitting on our relationship."

He thought we were in a relationship this whole time? That sounded like the sort of thing one of us should have said out loud. Words were impossible at that moment, but I'd let my actions say what I wanted. And I wanted Harry.

Taking his glass, I set both down gently. Then, hands on his shoulders, I pushed him back to the bedroom and shoved him onto the bed. I ripped his belt buckle apart, grabbed his slacks by the bottoms, and yanked them off. Then his trunks. I descended on his cock, filling my mouth with him to the back of my throat. He moaned and clutched at my hair, then pulled me upward with firm pressure. I kissed and licked everything on the way. Our tongues fought for dominance while he fussed with my belt and tugged my jeans and briefs down as far as he could reach. Chest to chest, erections grinding together, limbs fighting to hold the other nearer.

He rolled us over, standing only long enough to pull my jeans from where they twisted around my ankles. Kneeling behind my thighs, he pushed my knees up and apart, letting his cock's tip brush my hole while he took my length into his mouth. My eyes rolled back from whatever he was doing with his tongue.

I bucked and rolled us again. On top, I reached for the nightstand drawer, grabbing a rubber and the pump of lube. Seconds later, I was straddling him, reaching behind to stroke his cock, lining it up. He breathed slow and hard, puffing his cheeks with every exhale, eyes ensuring me it would be okay to stop if I couldn't do it. I leaned back, pushing his tip into me. The pressure burned and brought tears to my eyes, but I gently worked my cock at the same time, reminding my body that this would feel good.

"It's okay. Go slow," he whispered.

His hands on my hips, eyes on mine, Harry was a rock-hard statue beneath me, adding no surprises as I eased him in. Halfway there, I released, dropping my ass to his hips. We both gasped.

Yeah, this would feel good.

I held for another few breaths, savoring how he felt filling me, the pressure he applied in just the right places. I shifted up slowly, back down. Harry added to my rhythm, complimenting my upward movement by shifting down, pushing up to meet me halfway. He bit his lip, mouthing a drawn-out "Fuuuuuuck" when we sped up.

How long could my ass take this? I hoped it was at least long enough to feel him pumping his seed into me. Into the condom, but I'd still feel it.

Without pulling out, strong arms wrapped around me, and he tossed me to my back. Foreheads pressed together, slick with sweat, both puffing frantic exhales against the other's lips, Harry pressed into me with a smooth, steady gait. Every thrust slammed against that spot in my ass that threatened to make me cum without touching my dick.

"Does that feel good?" he gasped.

I moaned something that encouraged him to go faster, harder. His cock railed against the base of mine, sending shocks to the base of my skull. My balls tightened. I squeezed my eyes just as tight.

I had no other warning as I shot up my belly, to my chest. Harry's rhythm slowed to a concentrated push with the cords of muscle tensing in his neck. His cock pulsed in me. His gaze dropped down to mine, hair cascading down to frame his face while we both huffed for breath.

My arms flopped out to my sides. "Still doesn't prove you're not a prostitute." I leaned up to kiss the tip of his nose.

Harry kissed my lips again and held there to pull out. I gasped and clenched. Dismounting was always a shock.

He stood up on his knees, pushing back his hair. He looked perfect, his lean muscle outlined with the ideal amount of hair. His smile, though, slightly crooked, wrinkling his nose, got me more. "I'll get the sheet with all my payment options. I accept tap-to-pay now."

He let the deadpan joke hang long enough for me to doubt myself before dropping to my side with a chuckle.

I remember what I'd thought while fucking him just the other day, wanting to hurt him, watching myself in the mirror. Now Harry lay beside me, grinning and running his hand through my hair. Yeah, I wanted to start over with him, and this was a good way to do it.

Buzz Buzz

THREE WEEKS OUT OF a three-year relationship, I wasn't ready to commit myself to anyone for more than a night. Not that I had yet. Other than stolen glances in the gym locker room, I hadn't seen a naked ma,n other than my ex, in years.

It's time to change that.

And where better than Vegas?

I cycled between the apps, all bursting with a hundred guys active within a mile. All had their fair share of headless torsos, extremely confident older men, and obvious catfish. The rise of AI-generated images made that last category more difficult to identify. The few I messaged didn't respond, or we were spinning our wheels on an endless cycle of "Hey... Hey..." back and forth. Those who messaged me I either had no interest in or looked so far out of my league that I was sure their profiles were fake. I had no doubt there would be a number of sickos in Vegas that would try to lure in gays for... I didn't want to think about it.

Six hookup apps, and I couldn't find anyone. What was the point?

It was only the first night. I had plenty of time to find someone.

Dropping my phone on the charger, I rolled over and stretched out in the center of the king-sized bed. I'd forgotten how nice it was not to share a bed with someone on vacation. I only had a queen bed at home.

My phone buzzed twice.

I wanted to ignore it. I could just put my phone on silent and enjoy all the space in bed to myself.

It buzzed again.

Fuck. Curiosity wins.

Two messages from Jockbottom. Great name. So original. His profile picture looked believable, standing in front of the bathroom mirror with a shirt on, his phone and hands covering his face. 27, 6'1", 187 lbs, less than 100 feet away.

Hey cutie.

Are you at the Eclipse?

I rolled my eyes at the flattery but let it slide. I started half my dialogs the same way. And I was obviously in the Eclipse if we were that close—whatever, icebreakers.

Yeah, just settling in for bed.

It's nice being able to spread out.

I stared at my last line and realized how out of practice I was with flirting. I quickly added another.

Naked.

I didn't know if that would help, but I didn't care. It also wasn't true. I was wearing a pair of frumpy boxers. I was really out of touch from the scene.

Minutes passed, and I thought Jockbottom had given up on me, not that I'd blame him. I'd started to drift off when my phone buzzed.

Nice. Me too.

I waited for another message, but nothing came. Fuck it, go big or get no dick.

Show me

The image came in a few breaths later, a kind of blurry shot with lousy lighting of his chest down naked under the covers. Goddamn, I didn't think he'd actually do it, and if he did, I didn't expect him to be soft in the picture. That only made it hotter, more real. I was following the lines of his abs and trim waist when the message came in.

Your turn

Well, since you asked... I tore off my boxers, tossing them at the TV. After a quick debate, I chose an angle to include the tree tattoo along my side, snapping a shot just as bad as he sent me. Except I was at half-mast.

Send.

Of course, we were talking on the one app without an indicator showing the other person was typing. Luckily, his response came quickly.

Nice

Cool tattoo

Thanks. I have others. Maybe I'll show you.

Yeah? What do I have to do for that?

Send me another pic

He must have already been setting it up. He stood in front of the full-length mirror in his room with all the lights on, phone and hands covering his face like his profile picture. I zoomed in, tracing my eyes along his pecs, following the trail of hair down his abs, to his cock, now fully erect, and his balls hanging heavy below. I kept looking down his muscular thighs and calves, noting the tan line left by skimpy swimwear. Back to his dick, I zoomed in and thanked whoever created HD and 4k cameras. I could feel the texture of his short pubes through the screen.

My phone buzzed with another incoming message. Another shot, this time looking down his tight body, the angle close to his chest, one hand holding his cock, his bare feet blurry in the distance. His dick's head shone with the pressure of his squeeze.

Another. An upward angle from below his balls with his dick, oozing precum, blocking his face.

I was no photographer, but I did my best to recreate what he'd sent me. Tossing aside the sheets, I positioned myself in front of the mirror, glad for my post-breakup workouts. No, not enough. I dropped to a high plank for twenty quick pushups and flipped for a set of crunches before jumping back to my feet for a set of squats. It might not have made a difference, but here we go.

Snap. Send.

I didn't zoom in on my pic until after it was gone. Yeah, I looked pretty good. Muscle lines along my ribs and that V down my hips. I'd trimmed my pubes and shaved my balls before getting on the fight, so everything was looking neat and ready for interaction. I grabbed my cock at the base, squeezing tight as I aligned the next shot, making sure to get my feet. For the last, I mixed it up, squatting low with the phone on the floor to get my asshole in the frame.

Fucking nice

Incoming media, a closeup of his hole pulled open with his first and middle fingers.

I want that cock in me

Come get it. I'll pound you until you can't walk straight for a week.

Can't walk... The fuck did I just say? Also, that was a serious over-exaggeration of my skill and innate abilities.

More incoming media, this one taking longer to load because it was a video. Shot from the chest down, he lay naked on the bed with his knees wide. He stroked his cock a dozen times, then rubbed the head, pulling a strand of pre-cum with his finger. The app only allowed seven-second videos. I watched it loop three times, realizing I was touching myself and laid down to send him back the same thing. The background imagery was all the same; he might have been in an identical room next door. I had enough precum to rub down my dick from head to base, then back to the tip for more. I rarely needed lube when barebacking. After I hit send, it struck me that he ignored my invitation.

The next video was him rubbing lube onto a thick, dark rubber cock. He must have had a great time explaining that to TSA. The next was a closeup of the tip pushing into his ass.

Goddamn, I had nothing to send back to that. I'd been following his lead, mimicking his angles while he ignored my other offers, but I wasn't going to find something from the hotel room to shove up my ass.

I worked my cock, rubbing precum across the head. Send.

Held my fist on the edge of the room's desk, thrust into it, working my abs like a smooth wave. Send.

Hooking my thumb into my mouth, drawing it out slowly, careful not to get too much of my face. Send.

Incoming video... His phone's propped up on the sheets by his ankles. His knees are propped up and wide. He worked his cock with the dildo resting in his ass.

Incoming video... Phone in his hand, hard cock in the foreground while he furiously worked the dildo behind his balls.

Incoming video... He leaned over the desk, working the dildo.

> I could do better than that rubber. Room #?

Incoming image... A hand-scrawled note on hotel stationery, "CUM 4 ME." His hard dick was resting on the left side of the paper.

He had no intention of meeting. We'd probably see each other in a buffet line or share a blackjack table and never know.

Incoming video... Seven seconds of him jerking off over the note with his hand only a blur over a cock slick with precum or lube.

I watched it twice and sent back the same. After a half hour of toying and teasing, I was close. I paused just long enough to write my room number on a piece of stationery, starting the seven-second video with the first shot of cum across the desk. I hit send and started another to capture the last. I ran my hand through it, sending a still of cum dripping from my fingers.

He'd sent me three videos. Another of him furiously beating off. A closeup of cum pulsing from his head into his palm. Him rubbing the cum back over his cock in slow, languid strokes.

> Fucking hot

> [Message cannot be delivered]

It took me a moment to process what had happened, and then all I could do was snort and roll my eyes. Of course he'd fucking blocked me. Fuck this guy.

A worry crept in, making me regret giving him my room number. Maybe I could move rooms in the morning, say the shower was slow in this one. I worried less the longer I lay in bed. It was a standard exchange. I would have blocked him by now in most situations. I'd done it a dozen times on these apps. Trade digital cocks and cum for an hour, never to speak again.

The next night, after hours at the clubs where I only left with a stomach full of well vodka, I was sitting up in bed naked, room lit only by my phone's glow. I was ready to roll over to sleep when I heard a knock at the door. It was so faint I thought it might be down the hall, but I heard it again. I padded over with the only light from the peephole and crack under the door to guide me. Though the former, I spied an early twenties, clean-shaven man with close-cropped jet-black hair. He looked nervous in his tank top and cargo shorts, shifting weight between his feet and glancing down the hall.

"Who is it?" I asked.

His eyes flicked to the peephole and rather than saying anything, he held up a familiar piece of hotel stationery reading "CUM 4 ME."

Fuck!

No way he was 27, like his bio said. He barely looked old enough to drink, at least not legally. By the lean muscles of his arms and shoulders and hair peeking from the tank's swooping neckline, he certainly seemed like the guy I'd jerked off with last night.

"Just a sec." Obscenities flowed from me as I flicked on the lights and sprang back to the pile of clothes at the end of my bed, pulling on basketball shorts and a T-shirt. I checked my breath, then the peephole to make sure Jockbottom was still standing awkwardly in the hall before opening the door. He blinked up at me. Definitely not the 6'1" he promised, either. But damn if he didn't look great with his pecs popping as he passed me.

"Can I get you a drink?" I asked, closing the door, watching his bubble ass and toned calves walk deeper into my room.

"Sure." His voice was deeper than I expected, with an unfamiliar accent.

I took two hard ciders from the mini fridge, the last of my six-pack. He was sitting on the end of my bed when I turned to hand it to him. "Want to pick up where we left off last night?"

He took the bottle in one hand and a fistful of my chubbed cock with the other. His dark eyes locked on mine as he took a long drink while massaging my rapidly growing member.

Goddamn, so we were doing this.

I set my bottle on the table behind me and crept onto the bed, straddling him, groin to his chest. His hand never released as I moved, but he let his empty bottle roll from his fingers onto the comforter. Fucker drank the whole thing in one go. That hand slid up the leg of my shorts to cup my balls. I hissed from how cold his fingers were. I tugged his tank top up, forcing his hands off me long enough to get his arms free, then traced a palm down his pecs, relishing in the swirls of hair down his flat stomach. He had my shorts pulled down just enough to get a hand around my shaft, then leaned forward to lick the precum from my head.

Hands on his shoulders, I shoved him back and crawled up him with my cock in his face. He greedily took it, working his tongue, lips, and hand in quick, eager motions. I bridged my hips, going into a high plank over him, and thrust downward, savoring his moan and choke. Again and again, I pushed into him. His hands grabbed my bare ass, urging me faster and deeper.

I gave him what he wanted, shoving my cock down his throat. I wouldn't be cumming from this, but fuck if it didn't feel great, skullfucking a stranger in Vegas. No, I needed to see everything I saw last night.

He moaned his disappointment when I pulled out. Crawling back down him, I snapped the fly on his cargo shorts and pulled down as I went. I licked my way back up those heavy balls, curling my tongue behind them and up his cock. He only hit my tonsils four times before he pulled back his hips and scooted farther up the bed, raising and spreading his knees when he settled his head on my pillow.

I took the bait, rushing forward, aiming for his neatly shaved asshole. My tongue slid up his taint, and the gasp that escaped him when I blew across it spurred me on. I pushed into him and felt his back arch. Working back up to his cock, I caught his eyes, and they flicked to something behind me. I looked back. The hotel-provided intimacy kit was sitting beside the TV in a sealed bag.

Yeah, don't got to ask me twice.

Snagging it, I ripped it open, tearing the condom open with my teeth. Seconds later, I was kneeling between his thighs, squirting lube into my hand, rubbing it up my cock, then sliding it up his ass, fingering his hole. His eyes rolled up, and his head dropped back as I pushed in, keeping my pressure slow and even. I held there a moment, savoring his tightness, giving him a moment to adjust before sliding out fully and pushing back in, giving him a little extra with the last inch, tapping his head against the headboard. Again and again, a dozen times more, pulling all the way clear and ramming my way to his core.

Once I knew he could take it, that he was eager for more, I grabbed his knees from beneath, pulling his ass a few inches from the bed, and found my rhythm, staying in him as I worked. His hand found his cock, working it furiously while the other pinched a nipple.

Why was I still wearing a shirt? I ripped that off, tossing it across the room.

My body slick with sweat, I didn't know how much longer I'd last. I wanted to draw it out, flip him over, take him from behind. Lean him over the desk or against the wall. I wanted the front desk to call with a noise complaint.

He decided for us. Grunting between his gasps, his ass squeezed around my cock, but I held firmly in him. Cum burst from him, so unlike his video last night, landing across the hair on his belly and pecs. That sent me over the edge. Pushing myself fully into him, my balls clenched with that divine ache, holding firm until the last spasm. Pulling out, I peeled off the condom and tossed it at the plastic-lined garbage bin, not caring if it made it in.

I pushed up beside him, flopping to my side.

He took a moment to catch his breath, then rolled to me, grinning. "I'm Adam, by the way."

I snorted. "Liam. Nice to meet you."

Poker

Sy AND I HAD seen each other naked, but not since the summer after seventh grade. That was three months of us finding any excuse to take our pants off. It was never sexual, just raging hormones, curiosity, and a lack of parental supervision. Fifteen years later, Sy was back in town, and it was like no time had passed between us. In our catching up, I'd told him I'd come out and introduced my then-boyfriend Chet, whose dumbness was only balanced by the size of his dick.

The three of us went to a cheap dinner and back to Sy's little apartment. I remember the window to the courtyard was wide open and how clearly I could see into others' rooms, so how clearly they could see us. Sy poured us a stiff drink, asking what else we wanted to do. Chet suggested a movie, knowing Sy's bed was the only place to watch from. Chet wanted badly to see Sy naked after I admitted to him what we did as kids.

Sy had a better idea: poker. But not playing for chips.

"Strip poker, really?" I asked. "Are we all playing with the same number of chips? Do you still run commando?"

"I can start with a disadvantage." He winked and shuffled cards at his little dorm-size dining table. Chet was pulling up a chair with a giant grin on his face.

I should have fought for a different game because I'm terrible at poker. Though, even if you lose at it, you're still winning. We were playing with house rules that whoever won a hand would pick who would lose an article. A few hands in, it was clear Sy was targeting me. I sat in my briefs and one sock, the rest of my clothes in a pile beside me, and then I lost the sock. Chet won the next hand, then me, getting Sy to just his cargo shorts. Meanwhile, my hot, dumb boyfriend was still fully clothed. Yes, Sy definitely wanted me naked.

I held one pair. It was something, but probably not enough to win.

"You know, we could have just gotten naked and saved the preface," I said.

"Isn't this more fun?" Sy winked.

"I feel overdressed." Chet pulled off his t-shirt, stretching his arms overhead to show off the cords of muscle across his chest. Sy was watching, too.

"Show me what you've got, boys," said Sy, laying his cards out. "Two pairs."

"Fuck, one pair."

Sy looked between us with a predatory grin. "Who to pick?"

"Neither." Chet put down his cards. "Flush." He saved me, at least for the moment, or so I thought. "Off with them, Dave." He bit his lip to hold back his grin.

"Fucking traitor," I grumbled, lifting my ass just enough to slip off my trunks. I held them up for the others to see and dropped them on the pile.

"Don't be mad," Chet cooed, reaching under the table, sliding a hand up my thigh, slipping his hand around my half-chubbed cock, the end oozing precum. He brought his fingers to his lips, staring at Sy as he licked them.

"Keep playing, or skip to the end?" Chet asked.

Sy considered Chet a moment, then turned his attention to me, a wicked smile on his lips. "Could you get me another beer?" He jerked a thumb toward the kitchen behind him.

"Get it yourself."

"Come on, Dave," said Chet. "He asked so nicely."

"Fuck you both." I cupped my hands over my dick and stood. I wouldn't give up a show just yet.

I dropped my hands once I was past Sy, squatting low in front of his fridge to get a beer from the bottle drawer. I covered myself again before I turned, making it clear that I was rubbing my balls on the can's top.

Sy laughed. "Fucking asshole."

"It's so cold," I said with an exaggerated shiver.

My foot slipped, and I wheeled a hand to the counter to catch myself. I recovered, but there was no point in being coy after that. I slapped my cock on the beer's lid and handed it to Sy.

He shrugged, popped the top, and drained half the can in one drink, all without taking his eyes off my dick. "Your deal."

Chet won again and waggled an eyebrow at Sy. My old friend stood, shoulders drooped in mock defeat. "Well, boys, here you go." His fingers slid into his shorts, dropping down in a heartbeat. His fat cock hung plump from a nest of dark hair, and his balls looked like a whole handful. So much more than fifteen years ago. He sat down again.

That answered the why. He wanted to show off. I was no longer just half-chubbed.

"Do you want to see me naked?" Chet asked, rubbing a hand under his pec.

Sy flicked a glance at me, almost as if asking permission. I nodded back toward Chet.

"You want to watch Dave fuck me?" Chet asked, leaning forward to peek over the table's edge in front of Sy.

He didn't reply right away, so I stood, squeezing one hand around the base of my cock to make sure Sy was looking at it. He was, his lips parted slightly. Gesturing for Chet to stand, I slipped behind him, reaching around to unbutton his shorts and tug them to the floor along with his boxers.

In a deep squat with my boyfriend's ass in my face, I noticed the open window and distant neighbors but didn't care. Give them a show.

I stood, wrapping one hand around Chet's fat, uncut cock and the other across his chest.

"You want me to spread you out on this table?" I growled into Chet's ear, but my eyes were on Sy. His right hand was in his lap.

I pushed a hand into Chet's shoulder blades, and he leaned forward, bracing his hands on the table as his stance widened. My cock leaked precum like a bad faucet, and I smeared it across Chet's ass, pressing the tip against his hole.

I pressed harder, feeling myself slip in. Chet gasped, gripping the table's edges and arching his back.

Sy stood, one hand holding his cock and the other across his chest, pinching a nipple.

"Fuck me, Dave," Chet gasped and waved for Sy to get closer, to climb onto the table in front of him.

I pushed into Chet, sliding easily with my glut of self-lubrication. Slowly, out and back in. Again. He pounded the table with a fist and leaned to press his forehead against the grain.

Sy stood still with one hand on his dick.

"You wanna fuck him?" I asked. "Or let him take care of you while I do it?"

Chet flinched, but I might have only noticed, being inside to my balls. He relaxed again just as quickly. "Yeah, do it, Sy. Fuck me with that big dick."

That unfroze him. Sy stepped around the table, around Chet, as I slid out. With my boyfriend's face buried against the table again, Sy took me by the hand, placing it on his cock. His other slipped behind my neck, pulling me into a kiss. My lips parted for his tongue to move across mine. When he pulled back, his eyes showed what I was feeling. We'd wanted to do this years ago, fifteen years ago. My life flashed, wondering what we might be today if we'd been together rather than just boys playing with their dicks out.

Chet moaned, pulling our attention back to him.

I moved behind Sy, guiding his dick into Chet while I pressed mine between his legs.

"Goddamn, you're huge," Chet breathed with a giggle.

Sy craned his head back, finding my lips with his.

He pumped slowly, in and out to a moaning Chet, while I spread my precum across Sy's asshole. I wouldn't press it, but he stopped his motion just long enough to hold my dick at his entrance.

I wrapped my arms around his chest and pushed gently. My lips moved across his neck as my head slipped in. His fingers, laced through mine, tightened, squeezing as he pushed back into Chet.

For a moment, I didn't care about the open window or Chet moaning a few inches in front of me. The world was only me and my old friend Sy. I ground against him, feeling closer than I had to Chet for months, if ever. Sy locked his gaze on mine, and I saw a similar desire in him.

"You're gonna fucking make me cum!" Chet groaned through clenched teeth. "Fuck me hard! Cum in me!"

The moment broken, Sy focused forward, driving precise strikes into my boyfriend with enough violence that I couldn't stay in him. Chet gripped the far edge of the table, now fully lying across it as Sy pressed deep into him, legs locking up, shooting his load deep inside Chet.

Sy slipped out, pivoting to the side and pressing against my lower back, pushing me toward Chet spread out over the table. I leaned to kiss Sy again, but he glanced away. Sipping into Chet, now stretched by Sy's thick cock, I finished within a few thrusts and pulled out, my dick covered in both our seed.

"Fucking shit, wow." Chet pushed off the table, a poker card stuck with cum to his abs. He moved a finger through it and to his lips. "Thanks for inviting him in." Chet winked and passed between us, heading to the bathroom.

We watched until the door closed.

I rushed to fill the space between us, pressing my lips to Sy's. He pulled back after a hesitant second.

"What's wrong?" I asked.

"That was... Goddammit, Dave," Sy hissed. "That was amazing. If things were different, that would be us every night. We work. We always have."

"Then what?"

Sy waved at the bathroom door and the off-tune singing from behind it.

"Chet?" I asked. "What about him?"

Sy sat down hard with his elbows on his knees, hands gripping through his hair. "I'm not going to steal you away from your boyfriend."

I knelt between his feet to look up into his eyes. "Sy, Chet has been great to fuck the last four months, but you have to admit there was something real between us."

"There was." He leaned forward, brushing his lips against mine. "I've never been fucked. I never wanted to be. I didn't know it would feel so... connecting."

"Maybe it could just be us next time?"

"With Chet watching?" Sy gave a wry smile.

Would I leave Chet that night? Maybe become a thruple?

The bathroom door opened with a loud creak, and I jerked to my feet.

"Your turn, Dave. Clean up your dick, and we gotta jet. I have an early day."

I didn't want to leave Sy alone with Chet, but I couldn't give a reason out loud. I leaned over the sink, stroking the stickiness from my cock as best I could. Luckily, I'd shaved my pubes short earlier in the week.

When I came out, Chet was recounting the story of when I blew him in an Old Navy fitting room. Sy sat in a different chair with his clothes wadded in his lap.

"Ready?" Chet asked.

"Yep. Sy... I'll call you." I wanted to cross to him, knock the clothes away to straddle his lap, wrap my arms around his neck, and make out with him in front of the window, in front of my boyfriend. Instead, Chet took me by a pinkie, pulling me toward the door.

Chet slammed me with questions on the ride home. He assumed I was standing in the corner while Sy railed him. I admitted to rubbing my cock against Sy's hole, but nothing beyond that. Not the slow, easy slide in. Not the kiss we've been waiting fifteen years for. Not my last-second thoughts about how Sy might exist in my future. Truth, though, I'd leave Chet in a heartbeat if it meant being with Sy, but if a person leaves one for another, what stops them from doing it again? Sy shouldn't trust me if I did that.

I called Sy the next morning but got a text reply that he was busy at work. When Chet got home from his appointment, I met him in the hallway naked. He tore off his clothes and I leaned him against the wall, gently pressing into him. I thought of Sy, and I tried to kiss Chet tenderly as I rocked my hips against him, but he only grunted and pressed his head into the wall, leaning his hips back and growling for me to fuck him harder. I did. I fucked him harder and faster than I had before, not slowing as I came, then quickly pulled out and went to the bathroom. When I came out ten minutes later, Chet was watching TV in his boxers. He didn't give a shit.

Two more days of noncommital text respons-
es from Sy, and I was sure I'd fucked us up for
good.

The next day, I woke to Chet already gone for
work and a text from Sy.

> Sy: Did you talk to Chet about it?

> Me: It?

> Sy: *us?

I hadn't. I wasn't even sure what that meant.
Trying more with the three of us? I wanted to
a dozen times and had practiced the conversation in every shower, but I didn't know how to
start it other than to pretend it was a joke. My
phone buzzed.

> Sy: ?

> Me: Can you come over at 1?

> Sy: {thumbs up}

Chet wouldn't be home until 2, giving us an
hour to devise a plan. Or to make slow, pas-
sionate love. I was just thrilled to finally have a
response from Sy.

He was a few minutes early, and I barely had the door closed behind him before our tongues were in each other mouths, and he'd gotten his shirt off.

"I want you, Dave," he gasped while working at my belt. "I haven't thought about anything else the last three days. I need you." He thrust his hand down my front. I gasped when he grabbed my swelling cock.

Slipping my fingers around his waistband, I pulled him to the bedroom.

The next hour rushed back in a wink. Somehow, neither of us came as we explored each other with fingers and lips. He hovered over me, knees between my thighs, hands planted by my armpits, working his way up my chest, leaving kisses in his wake.

"Hey, I'm home. You have company?"

I froze. We both did. We knew Chet would be home in an hour but had done nothing to stop before he did. No alarms set; no one watching the time.

"Oh..." Chet said from the bedroom doorway. Sy didn't move from where he hovered over me, looking under his arm at my boyfriend's confused face. His fingers moved to unbutton his work shirt. "I wondered if this would happen. Is there room for me?"

Room for him in the bed or the relationship? I sensed a double meaning, but I didn't think Chet would be bright enough to intend that.

"We've been waiting for you," I half lied and beckoned him to join.

He dropped his shirt and started at his belt buckle. Fuck, he looked good naked. "Did you guys get everything settled between you?"

Maybe Chet wasn't as dumb as I thought. I shared a glance with Sy, unsure if we had resolved anything.

Sy rolled off me as Chet climbed onto the side of the bed. "What if you were both inside me? I could do it if you're slow enough."

"Slow? You?" I grinned.

"I'd give it a try." Chet bit his lip. "If you two want to have a thing, I'm okay with that. Just tell me if things change for me."

Chet's sheepish vulnerability chilled me with guilt. He knew and saw more than I gave him credit for. Chet took one of my hands, then reached for one of Sy's in the other.

Only Fair

"YOU WANT TO SEE mine?" I asked from the door.

Corey stood at the bed's side with his shorts around his ankles. He'd teased me for weeks leading up to our trip to New Orleans, telling me how he'd show me his dick and offering to let me join in with any of the guys he picked up from the apps. We'd known each other for years, and by how much he talked about his game, I found myself a little underwhelmed seeing his dick for the first time. Not that there was anything at all wrong with what he was packing. Perfectly average size, with pubes shaved so close, they might be waxed.

He tugged on his dick and nodded at me.

It felt weird to show myself to someone else, like comparing weiners with a friend in elementary school. I'll show you mine if you show me yours, but that didn't stop me from dropping my shorts and trunks.

Corey made a humming noise, shuffling closer. "Nice," he said.

Unsure of what happens next, I offered, "Touch it if you want."

He glanced up at me through long lashes and moved nearer, slipping his cool fingers around my balls. How was he so cold in the New Orleans heat? It didn't matter. It felt nice. I grasped his length, squeezing gently and feeling it stiffen with each heartbeat. My blood thundered in my ears, and it wasn't until Corey raised a thumb to his tongue that I realized I was fully hard, leaking precum.

"Shit, sorry." I dipped my hips back, pulling away from him.

"Nothing to be sorry about." He slowly stroked himself.

I blew out a puff of air and reached for my shorts around my ankles. Not that Corey was in any way unattractive, but I never felt the desire to have sex with him. Tell that to our raging erections pointing at each other, I know.

He pulled up his shorts as I refastened my belt.

Corey threw himself across the king-sized bed, ass popped in the air, reaching for his phone on the nightstand. "What do you want to do tonight? Drinks? Strip bar? Random hookup?" His thumbs flew across his phone as he spoke, punctuated by the buzz of incoming messages. "This place is hot. Check this guy out." He rolled to his back.

I crawled across the bed to lie beside him. He shoved his phone toward me, the screen dominated by a gorgeous torso in a mirror selfie. All the stats along the side put him at just over average height, below average weight, versatile, and well-endowed. I had no doubt that Corey's profile was nearly identical.

"Does he have any other pics?" I asked.

Corey's phone buzzed, and he showed me the new image. Headless-torso-man held the phone close to his bare chest, snapping downward with his thumb in his boxer's waistband. He was hot. Flat stomach, thighs that made the green plaid boxers tight, and a bulge that made them tighter.

"Should I show him my dick?" Corey asked, grinning.

I chuckled and rolled to the bed's edge. "Do what you gotta do. I gotta pee."

He unzipped and pulled himself free, still hard from our moment. My bladder urged me to ignore him, at least for this moment. We had four nights in New Orleans. If we continued at this pace, I'd be sick of seeing Corey naked by the end of it.

In the bathroom, I briefly considered setting up a quick profile on each of the apps, just to browse and see what the city had to offer. No... I needed more than a pic and some stats. I needed to see the guy in motion at a bar or club. Old fashioned, I know.

Corey cursed from the bedroom. Not loud enough to signal a true emergency, but I still hurried. He sat propped up on his elbows when I opened the door, dick stashed away but shorts unzipped.

"What's wrong?" I asked, lying beside him on the bed.

He showed me his phone with a well-framed close-up of his hairless dick. It was a master-piece, making him appear far larger than I knew him to be. "Very nice." I blinked at the phone's brightness.

He still held up the image. "Look at the top-left."

Looking past his pale cock, there I was, blurred in the background.

"He wants to see you, too."

I scoffed. "Tell him I don't show off to random headless guys. I'm a slow burn." I licked a finger and dragged it down my chest with a sizzle. "It took you how long to get my pants off."

Corey pulled his phone away and went back to tapping. "I could have gotten you quicker if I tried."

"What a shame you never tried with me." I rolled my eyes.

"Wanna make a bet?"

"It's a bit late for us."

"No, this guy." He pointed to his phone.

"He's already seen your dick. Wait, what are we betting on?"

"He doesn't know which of us is who in the pic I sent. If I can get him to come over, we'll see who can get him naked first."

"And how can we determine that if we're both in the room with him?"

"Fine, fair. Whoever touches his cock first is the winner."

"I don't know, Corey. I plan on getting my dick wet while we're here, but sex bets are a little weird."

He put his hand on my chest, shaking me. "Come on, it'll be fun."

"What are we playing for? What do I get when I inevitably win?"

"Winner gets the king bed. The loser has to sleep in the other room."

I expected to be on the pull-out all week; there was no losing for me. "Deal."

Corey pumped a fist and got back to tapping on his phone. I got up to find an outfit to wear out tonight. He'd have his guy over while I enjoyed the nightlife of drinking, dancing, and making out with a stranger in the park. Then I'd come back to Corey on the couch with this guy and a bottle of tequila, him still trying to come up with the nerve to touch his arm.

"Fuck! He can be here in twenty minutes!" Corey jumped up and ripped through his bags. "I have to clean out and shower."

"Clean out? I thought you were a top."

"That's what all vers bottoms say," he said on the way to the bathroom. He didn't bother closing the door as he stripped and sifted through his toiletry bag. "His name's Luke." I saw the anal bulb in his hand, and he closed the door.

I expected hours of them going back and forth to work out something. If he actually showed up, Corey would have plenty of time to win the bet. I still got up and got dressed in a nice shirt and jeans. The shower had only shut off when someone knocked twice. The guy through the peephole could definitely have the body I'd seen in those pics, so I opened the door. His black hair was shaved on the sides and pulled into a knot on top. He looked poured into his tight tank top and jeans. Luke put a hand on the door frame, chewing gum and staring at me with eyes as dark as his hair.

"Hey," I said and backed up for him to enter the rented apartment.

Luke stepped in, leaning against the wall opposite me, stretching an arm behind his head to casually show off his bicep. "Nice place," he said without looking away from me. "Your friend here?"

I heard movement from the bedroom. "Yeah, he's in there."

His eyes flicked that way, then back at me, loudly chewing his gum. Maybe I did want to stick around and see his guy in action, plus it sounded like they might be in need of a top.

No, I wanted my night out. But first... I stepped close to Luke. "Let me touch your dick. Right now."

His eyes widened, but he smiled around chewing his gum and nodded. "You get right to it. Nice." Luke took my hands and set them on his belt buckle. "Go for it."

Goddamn, I didn't expect that to work. I yanked open his belt, flicked the top button of his jeans, pulled down his zipper, and plunged my hand down Luke's front. With balls and a shaft as smooth as I could ever hope for, he wasn't hard yet, but getting there.

"Really, dude?" Corey said with a huff. He stood in the bedroom doorway, wearing only a white towel.

Luke slipped a hand down my jeans, grabbing my girth as it pumped back to attention.

I pulled my hand free and brought it to my nose for a deep sniff. Despite the New Orleans heat and humidity, he smelled as clean as if he'd just gotten out of the shower across the hall. "Why don't you get comfortable in the bed-room? In my bedroom?"

Luke removed himself from my pants and licked a finger. He grabbed Corey's crotch as he passed him.

My friend watched him go and rushed to me. "That doesn't count!"

"Uh, I think it does. Be careful; he feels thick. Don't make a mess on my bed."

Corey noticed my jeans and nice shirt, eying me up and down. "Going somewhere?"

"I didn't come to New Orleans to get ass Door Dashed to me. I'm hitting a few bars. Tell Luke I'll give him another round if he's still here when I get back." I said it, but didn't turn to leave. I watched the bedroom doorframe, debating what I actually wanted out of the night. Corey grabbed my shirt, twisting me to face him.

"You gotta stay, Mal. Please. I told him he'd get us both."

"Then this'll be a lesson not to offer my dick without asking first."

He tugged at my shirt, pleading up at me with puppy eyes. "Fine, you won the big bed. What else do you want? I'll do your laundry when we get back; how about that? I promise we'll go out tomorrow."

When would I next get the chance for a friend to beg me to fuck another guy? We had a nice bottle of tequila here. The bars were just loud and expensive. "Fine. But we're going to do this my way."

Corey clapped, but his joy quickly soured. "Wait, what does that mean?"

"You'll find out," I winked. "Get the tequila."

He nodded, shrinking away from me toward the kitchenette.

I didn't know what I meant, either, but I delighted in watching him squirm.

I stepped into the bedroom doorway as Luke was closing the nightstand drawer. Nosey fuck. Luckily, this was a rental with nothing of interest except for maybe a bible. So... nothing of interest. Wait, no. I'd seen Corey dump the rubbers and lube in there. Luke sat on the bed and lay on his side, propped on his elbow.

"You're the one in command, then," he said in a deep growl. "Are you going to tell me what to do as I fuck your boyfriend?"

Rolling my shoulders back, I cracked my knuckles and crossed to him, leaning over with a knee on either side of his legs, and grabbed his top knot. "That's right," I growled back. "I'm the one in charge here. I tell you when to beg for more, when you've had enough, and don't you even think about cumming without my saying you may."

I let go, and he fell back with a gasp, but his lip curled up just a fraction.

Corey entered with the bottle of tequila in one hand and a stack of cups in the other.

"Looks like you boys are already getting it started," he said, crossing to the bed and mounting it on his knees, crawling toward Luke. It was a small miracle that his towel didn't fall off.

"I was just giving Luke the rules," I said, smiling down at the stranger with a feral grin. Honestly, I couldn't stop and explain why I was acting this way, but fuck if I wasn't more turned on than I had been in recent memory.

"Oh?" Corey sat back on his heels and poured out a cup of tequila, handing it to Luke. "What are the rules?"

"That you both do what I say, when I say it."

Luke pushed up on his palms, licking his lips. "Tell me what to do." He knocked back the tequila in one go.

I crawled up on Luke, leaning forward so our noses nearly touched. His erection stabbed my ass even through our jeans. "You're going to eat my friend's ass until your tongue is ready to fall off. Then you're going to fuck him until he can't remember his mother's name. Got it?"

Luke's dark eyes widened, but his lip curled upward, and he nodded.

I twisted his top knot in a fist. "Say, 'yes sir.'"

He swallowed hard, eyes drilling into mine. "Yes, sir." His voice quaked.

I fell forward, crushing him with a violent kiss that surprised even me, my tongue forcing through his lips to tangle with his. I pushed back just as suddenly, wiping the back of my hand across my mouth and working my way backward to stand at the edge of the bed, knees on either side of Luke's legs dangling off. Corey stared at me with a stunned, wide gaze, the bottle in one hand and two quarter-full cups in the other.

Luke pushed back to his palms and drew his feet up from between my legs. I took a cup from Corey and stepped back to shift an arm-chair closer. "Begin," I said, sitting with one knee tossed over the armrest and waved between them.

Luke shook his head and focused on Corey without any of the gum-chewing calm he'd shone at the door. He popped up to crawl on all fours across the bed, settling back on his heels, tracing the back of his hand down Corey's arm, moving it around his lower back, and leaning forward to kiss. Corey's hands cupped Luke's cheeks for a few breaths before sliding down to tug at the hems of his tank top. Jealously spiked in me, watching Corey move across the stranger's broad shoulders and how the hair trimmed short across his pecs traced a line down his flat stomach. How one hand cupped behind the other's neck and the other hand disappeared down the back of Luke's jeans.

"Eat his ass," I demanded.

They both glanced at me, then Luke took Corey by the hips, flipping him over and ripping away his towel. Both hands spread Corey's cheeks, and he plunged forward. My friend's back arched as he caught himself from toppling forward with a gasp. Luke attacked, pushing deep, shoving Corey forward, coming up only long enough to breathe and drag his tongue up my friend's taint. I saw a glint of light from the drop of precum on Corey's cock just before he buried his face in the sheets and ran his hands through his hair.

Luke hooked Corey's leg, flipped him to his back, and tossed his legs over his shoulders. He didn't waste a second before diving back in and pushing Corey's hips up.

I could have cum from the sight of it. I'd seen it a thousand times in porn, but now I was the director.

And directors gave notes.

"Put a finger in him."

Luke sank his middle finger into his mouth, drawing it out slowly, leaving it wet, and pushing it into Corey without hesitation. Working to the second knuckle, then all the way in, Luke leaned to take Corey's smooth cock in his mouth, pumping his neck with the same timing as his finger. It was a nice bit of improv, but not what I wanted in that moment. And as the director, I'd get what I want.

"None of that," I said, and Luke's head snapped up. "Neither of you will touch his dick."

Corey's eyes were wide, pleading at me. Too bad. You wanted this, so you were going to let me try something new.

Luke dropped back to Corey's ass, working his tongue while his middle finger pumped. He pulled out, put his index finger in his mouth, then pushed them both into Corey's ass. My friend moaned, but Luke's cock would be bigger.

"Tease him," I said.

"Yes, sir," said Luke, rising to his knees and working his fly. His cock flopped into his fist, eight thick inches of uncut beauty. He stroked it twice, then pivoted slightly toward me, providing me a full view. I downed what was left of my tequila to keep myself from drooling. Luke focused back on Corey, but glanced my way as he pushed his cock against my friend's ass, letting his length and girth slide up the crack, teasing the hole for what was about to come.

I sat back in the chair, not realizing how I'd been leaning forward. "The drawer." I nodded at the nightstand. Luke pulled free of Corey and crawled up the bed. He knew what was there, thanks to his snooping. His hard length flopped with the movement and he struggled to shed his jeans without wasting time. Taking a condom from the top drawer, he expertly ripped the package open and had it rolled onto his dick within seconds. Walking on his knees back to Corey, he dribbled lube from the travel-sized bottle into his palm. My friend licked his lips, breathing hard with anticipation.

Luke pushed Corey's knees up and positioned himself but turned to me. "How do you want me to do it?"

I wasn't completely sure why I wanted my friend to suffer. "Slow. Make him beg for it."

Luke nodded and sucked his teeth. With his big cock in his fist, he pushed forward achingly slow. Corey's head fell back, mouth agape. I knew that feeling, not wanting it rushed at first, but then it should speed up, get a little rougher. Not tonight. Only slow.

Our boy couldn't have been in more than a third of the way before he pulled out just as slowly. Luke tapped his cock on Corey's balls twice and lined up for another run. But first, his gaze dropped over his shoulder, locked on mine. His eyes dropped to my crotch spread wide.

His eyebrows flicked, and his hips eased forward. Corey's breath caught.

Luke worked him, hands on my friend's thighs, but his eyes never left me, making it clear what he wanted.

And fuck, I wanted it, too. Watching him waiting for me to join and why shouldn't I? I slid a hand across the bulge in my jeans, squeezing my shaft. Luke's eyes lifted as if peeking into my lap.

Yeah, sure, of course. You can see it. That's only fair.

I did it slowly, pinching the zipper and drawing it down one tooth at a time. With the belt and button popped open, I traced a finger along the seams on my trunks, my hand disappeared into my jeans. Luke's eyes were wide. He nodded. I had every ounce of this man's attention even as he kept his slow rhythm in my friend.

"Harder, please," Corey moaned.

"Not yet," I said, not taking my attention from Luke. With my hand down my underwear, I gave my cock one more squeeze as if rallying it for the attention it was about to get. Not that it needed a rally; I was harder than a frat boy losing at beer pong with his brothers.

Working through the fly in my trunks, I brought out my cock for Luke to see, stretching it downward once, then letting it slap against my stomach. Luke wetted his lips and nodded his approval. Despite my orders, his pace increased, and I worked myself at the same rate, imagining how it felt for my friend while watching it happen. Watching Luke's body flow with his movement, the muscles along his back, his sides, his arms. How his ass clenched and relaxed.

Corey whimpered.

"Finish it," I said.

"Yes, sir," Luke said. He bit his lip, eyes still on me, and pushed upward, lifting Corey's ass from the mattress. I couldn't tell if my friend was in pain, but his screams didn't last long. He shot up his stomach, hitting himself in the chin in less than a minute. Luke slowed but didn't lose the intensity when his back arched, and we finally lost eye contact for a moment. He pumped twice more and fell forward, head on Corey's stomach, barely missing the strands of cum. Luke pivoted to watch me.

I don't know what tell I had, but Luke pulled out of my friend and nearly fell off the bed, dropping between my knees to catch the first of my load, shoving my cock to the back of his throat, working me fast without letting a drop spill.

When I finally calmed, he rose to kneel before me, eyes locked on mine. The light caught him just right to highlight the flecks of gold at the edge of his irises. My heart melted into those eyes as they neared, and then he kissed me. Light and gentle. The kind of kiss that took my breath with him when he pulled back.

"Whoa! That was great!" said Corey, rolling his legs off the bed and running a hand through his mess of hair. He stood, caught himself on the edge of the bed, and tried again on wobbly legs. He squeegeed a hand up his front to catch the cum from running. "Be right back." He winked down at Luke on his way to the bathroom.

Luke jumped to his feet, ripped the condom from his limp dick, and tossed it in the bin while searching for his clothes. "Let me see your phone," he said to me.

A bit stunned, I did, unlocking it with my fingerprint as I passed it over.

His thumb flew over the screen, and he tossed it back to me so he could dress.

"If you get some time alone, I'm free tomorrow night," he said, frowning at the sound of the toilet flushing. "I'd like you to tell me how to spend it."

"Yes, sir," I said.

He bent to kiss me again and fled the bedroom. The hall door closed a second later.

The bathroom door behind me opened. "How about some more sh... Did he leave?" Corey stood naked a few feet from me, fists on his hips.

I glanced at my phone and the new contact, then quickly tucked it away. "Said he had something to get to," I lied.

"Fuck." He stomped over to where his phone was on the bed and repeated his curse, showing me his screen. "Fucker blocked me. Isn't that typical? Pump and dump. Bet his name wasn't even Luke."

The new contact in my phone was under the name "Oli," but I wasn't going to mention that.

"Why don't you put on some pants, and we'll go for a drink?" I offered.

"Yeah..." he trailed off, letting his phone slip from his fingers and bounce on the comforter. "If that's what my director tells me to do," he winked.

Beach Day

A GRIN CREPT ACROSS my lips, watching Quinn slather sunscreen across his upper thighs, taking extra care with his dick and balls.

"Thank you for this," I said.

"Uh-huh." He adjusted his sunglasses and settled back into the longue chair.

"Of all the things we've done, I thought this would be right up your alley."

"Well," Quinn flopped his head dramatically toward me and pulled his glasses down. "You thought wrong." He pushed them back in place using his middle finger and returned to staring at the waves breaking a few dozen feet away.

The occasional person or couple walked between our canopy and the water line. Most were old enough to be my grandparents, with leathered skin, tits and nuts sagging, but I only saw beauty in their wrinkled forms. What would it be like to have such confidence at their age? Maybe they just stopped caring.

An ancient couple passed near our umbrella, the man frowning down at Quinn and me the whole time. The woman said something as they were walking away. I couldn't understand most of it, but I would swear I heard her use the f-slur. I shrugged it off. The hateful old fucks would be dead soon.

Quinn had in his ear buds, listening to his smut audiobooks no doubt, so I leaned back with my paperback. I must have dozed off because next I knew, I was jolted awake.

"Pardon me, boys," asked the nude man at the foot of my chair. He was skinny and pale, with dark tattoos inked from his left armpit all the way down to his ankle. "Oh, sorry, I didn't mean to wake you."

I sucked in a deep breath and shook my head. "I just dozed off," I said. "Do you need something?"

Beside me, Quinn stretched an arm and let it lay across his groin, obscuring himself from the stranger.

The man raised the drawstring canvas bag in his left hand. "Would you mind watching my bag for a minute while I go in the water?" Oh, that accent... Italian...?

I sat up straighter, knees wide to straddle my chair with my feet in the sand. "I don't think anyone would touch your stuff, but sure." I waved to the space by my foot.

"Thanks, mate." He took a step into our shade, dropped his bag, and flashed me a grin. He winked at Quinn before turning toward the water.

"Nice ass," said Quinn when I hoped the stranger was out of earshot. "A bit skinny, but that only makes his dick look bigger."

I snorted.

"What?"

"What's this?" I clasped both hands over my genitals, mirroring him.

"What about it? He didn't need to see me."

"We've had sex with four men in the last week, but you want to remain modest with this guy?"

Quinn shrugged. "We're not having sex with him."

"Not yet, at least."

"That's right."

A few seconds of silence hung between us before I asked, "Would you want to have sex with him?"

Quinn hummed. "I wouldn't mind a closer look at those tattoos."

"We could find a quiet spot in the tall grasses at the sand's edge," I said, squinting into the water's glare. I spotted our stranger as he dove into the breaching waves. "It's your turn to top."

"It's always my turn to top, and I always pass." Quinn sat up, mimicking my posture, his knees wide and feet in the sand. "What about those changing rooms back there? They're out of the sun, no sand, with just the illusion of privacy."

"I bet he's straight."

"Everyone can be convinced," Quinn chuckled. "He could follow us to the changing room. He'll act surprised to see us in there; we notice how his eyes slide across our bodies, how he's grinning. You say you're going to take a shower in the open-air stall and come back to me riding him on the bench. You act shocked, offended, and demand justice. He offers to suck your fat cock, so we arrange it so that I'm riding him while he blows you, and I eat your ass."

"You want to eat my sunscreen-lathered ass after I'm been sweating in the sun for how long?"

"That's why you shower first."

"You've got it all worked out."

I watched Quinn for a long breath as he stared out at the ocean with unfocused eyes. I leaned forward a few inches to see him standing at full attention. A bead of precum glistened on his head.

"Why leave the beach?" I asked. "You could ride him right here. When the cute Mexican twink comes to ask if we want another chair, maybe he'd join us, too."

Quinn scrunched his nose. "He was too skinny."

"So is that guy in the water," I chuckled.

"But his tattoos are hot. So is that accent."

"Well, get that charm ready; he's coming back. You might want to put that thing away." I nodded at his erection.

"Fuck!" Quinn squirmed to cover himself with his hands but couldn't find a position that looked natural.

I adjusted my chubbed cock, laying it toward my hip. "Think of the queen and the Virgin Mary, right?" I watched our stranger at the water's edge, pushing back his hair with his face toward the sun.

"Fuck you," Quinn growled.

"Love you, too. Come on, wave around that boner. It'll be a good conversation starter."

"Did I mention fuck you?" Quinn started fighting with his chair, trying to get it to lay flat.

I let him struggle and watched our guy scanning across the beach, then start walking directly toward us, taking long strides up the incline to high tide's line of seaweed debris. He had no shame, bits shifting with each step, but I focused more on how his lean muscles tensed. My husband wanted this guy's dick in his ass, but I wanted to feel his arms, dig my fingers into his back, stroke his legs.

Quinn gave up with another string of curses and flopped on his back. He stretched his dick downward with two slow strokes and let it slap back onto his stomach. "Whatever."

I did the same, flexing my cock as I pulled it, squeezing the hard girth. Our guy could take his bag and go, but maybe he'd stay a moment to chat.

He combed his fingers through his dark hair as he approached. It was a lot longer than I first thought when he woke me up. I quickly imagined running my knuckles through it, tugging just enough to make him gasp.

He was all smiles as he stepped into the shade of our umbrella. "Thanks, mates." He dropped to a wide-knee squat to dig through his bag for a wire hair brush. "I can save your spot if you want to take a dip."

"I don't swim in salt water," said Quinn.

Our stranger made no attempt to hide how he stared at our erections while brushing out his hair, and I had a hard time taking my eyes off his growing as he spoke. "Looks like you boys are enjoying the day."

"Perfect weather, and I'm enjoying the view," said Quinn, tugging at this cock. What a difference to the shy persona of a few minutes ago.

I rolled my eyes at him. "We could fit another chair under here... I'm sorry. I'm Benj; this is my husband, Quinn."

"Willem," he said. "And thank you. I'd love to stay a bit, but I was just passing through, killing some time before my flight."

"Heading home?" Quinn asked.

"No," said Willem with an odd finality that stopped any follow-up questions. "Pleasure meeting you both. I'll just rinse off the ocean and be on my way." He rose, touching Quinn's knee as he did, giving it a squeeze.

"You want to hang out until that settles down?" I asked, pointing at his cock. I was only a few inches from being able to touch it.

Willem chuckled. "Maybe, but I don't think that'll happen on its own with the energy in here."

"We could all think about the queen and Virgin Mary," Quinn added with a slow jerk-off fist motion.

Willem bit back his grin and nodded.

"Maybe not here. Thanks again, gents. Hopefully, I'll see you around sometime soon." He passed between us on a direct line to the changing huts huddled at the sand's edge.

Quinn rolled to his side, watching Willem disappear into the hut. "We're following him, right? This is happening, yes?"

"We paid for the umbrella and chairs for the day; it seems a shame to waste them when we only just got here," I said. "But it's a shame to waste all these perfectly good erections."

We had everything shoved into our bag and were on our way to the hut in under a minute. We turned the corner to a room nine or ten feet on a side with a bench running through the middle. The hiss of water came from around the corner. No doors, no locks. Anyone could walk in, but that kind of danger only spurred me forward.

Without pausing any longer, I went first. The space, a quarter the size of the first room, didn't have a ceiling but had four shower heads, as if they expected that many people to realistically be in here at once.

Willem looked up from where he stood under the water's stream, stroking his cock. "Hey, gents."

"Room for two more?" Quinn asked. He didn't wait for an answer, but stepped into Willem's water, slipping a hand around his hip. Their heights were a perfect match for Willem to take both their cocks in his fist and continue stroking. Willem's eyes found mine as he leaned to kiss my husband, their lips and tongues trying to work out what the other liked.

I wouldn't be left out. I moved behind our stranger, grinding my cock into his ass and nuzzling my nose into his neck. His smell was intoxicating: some mixture of pricey aftershave, island sunscreen, and sweat. The harsh spray of the beach shower beat against my face, but it felt great sliding my hands down the man's lean muscles, down his ribs, around his firm ass cheeks.

With uncharacteristic generosity, Quinn said between breaths, "I want to watch you fuck my husband." I couldn't remember when last he directed a dick away from himself.

Willem said nothing, just turned in place to me, smirked, and put his hands on my shoulders to pivot me from him. I didn't resist, leaning forward to put my forearm on the wall and resting my head on it. Willem dropped to a squat, spread my ass, and plunged his tongue forward. He worked fast, pushing hard, making me gasp and moan with each redoubled effort. My knees weakened, and I widened my stance. I could have cum from just that and raised a hand to my cock, but it was immediately slapped away. Looking down, I saw Quinn sitting on the cement floor in front of me.

Willem stood, ran a finger up my taint to tease my hole, and I felt his fist working to align his cock. Fuck I hope he had enough natural lube—

He shoved forward, filling me, driving me into the wall, stealing my breath. Quinn worked my cock as only he could, giving me another focus as Willem held me in place.

He pulled out slowly...

Then thrust until I felt his hips flat again my ass.

Quinn did his magic, distracting me from the pain as it slowly turned to pleasure. Willem kept his belly pressed against my lower back, moving only his hips. He was so nearly hitting—

Quinn slid a finger in beneath Willem's cock, knowing exactly where to press within me. Any lingering worries of someone walking in on us were blasted away with the string of obscenities I screamed.

Our tattooed stranger pulled back, digging his fingers into my hips, slamming me fast and hard, driving my head into the wall.

Any thought was impossible. I knew I couldn't last long like this with Quinn working me inside and out and Willem railing me harder than I had been in recent memory.

Just when I was ready to tap out or blast my load, Willem's hands slid up my sides, gripping around my shoulders to hold his chest tight to my back. With a final thrust, his cock surged, pumping his seed into me. I fell within seconds, and Quinn was there to catch it. I fired down his throat, knees weakening further until I was on the verge of collapse.

Willem dropped behind me, tongue lashing out for his cum dripping from my ass. He fell onto Quinn next, finishing him quickly and swallowing the load.

The three of us slumped into a puddle under the water's spray, slowly regaining our breaths.

By the time I trusted my legs, I heard voices just around the corner—men speaking in tones barely audible over the water. Quinn pulled me up, and Willem was gone, having slipped away while I collected my wits.

Quinn and I acted casual as two leathered old men entered, speaking rapid Spanish. They nodded at us and continued their conversation.

Back in the room with the bench, we didn't have towels but pulled on our dry swimsuits. Something poked my thigh as I pulled mine up. Quinn and I took black business cards from our pockets at the same time. "La Luce" was scripted in a white serif font along with a +356 country code number. We held them up to each other with a shrug.

"Maybe Willem's inviting us to follow," said Quinn.

Also By Dirk

Other works by Dirk Mourningwood
La Luce's Legacy (2024)
Eros Unzipped (2024)
Eros Unchained (2024)

About Dirk

Dirk Mourningwood is an emerging voice in the world of MM erotica, known for his bold storytelling and captivating characters. With a passion for exploring the depths of human desire and the complexities of male relationships, Dirk weaves tales that are both sensual and emotionally resonant. His writing invites readers into a world where passion knows no bounds and love transcends all barriers. When he's not crafting his next tantalizing story, Dirk enjoys immersing himself in period dramas, practicing kenjutsu, and playing disc golf with his lab Rodger.